Antlers.

Eryk Salvaggio

Antlers

ISBN: 0692979344
ISBN-13: 978-0692979341

For V., regardless.

ANTLERS.

ACKNOWLEDGMENTS

Sections of this book draw on historical accounts of Itako, a Shinto-influenced folk tradition of blind female necromancers.

Soren Fox, Esquire.

1. FOX LAW

Nobody could say when the seals stopped sunning on Seal Rock. It was well before that other great disappearance, when the humans and the cats had faded from existence while everything else was looking away.

The sun had coaxed tiny droplets of water from the surface of the ocean to suspend themselves in the air. They floated there, gracefully expanding toward the shore and over the hills. When the fog broke, the humans and the cats were gone. The tide crashed around a jutting crag a few paces from the shoreline, as they always had. Then, in slippery grey flashes, the seals returned to their eponymous perch.

Years later, Soren Fox, Esquire, bid good morning to the fog as he made his way to work. The fog seeped beneath his rusty ginger fur, charging his skin with a sensation of cold electricity. Sorrel horses loitered on the street for anyone needing their service, but Soren preferred to walk. An employee of the court, he considered morning constitutionals his civic duty. He wanted to be in touch with those he served.

The foxes had organized the world in imitation of humans. They unified the entire living world under new laws based on years of close observation. Fox Law was the language that made dreams expressible, and Soren, a lawyer, was one of its most earnest gatekeepers.

The garbage continued to emerge on Tuesdays, sustaining the patterns that felt most comfortable for scavenger types. The Victorian homes held together as animals inherited a proclivity for urban life. Streets elegantly crumbled into wide grass thoroughfares. Soil, cooler and softer on the new occupants' paws, was trampled with the to-and-fro of pushcarts carrying wares from kitchens. Raccoons in yellow hats and raincoats peddled fishes fresh from catches in the surrounding seas.

Soren loved the rhythm of this city. He loved descending a hill into a neighborhood, watching the microcosm of shops and homes and schools expand as he grew closer. He loved to then ascend another peak and see the whole place laid out for him, as if in miniature. He never felt very far from being submerged into something familiar, or reminded of its part in the greater thing.

Badgers and fox-kits bounced a kick-ball in the courtyard. A badger boy shot one over the fence to land near Soren, and called for him to return it.

Soren, the youngest of five brothers, was familiar with athletic inferiority and threw it twice as far as he needed in overcompensation. Four badger boys scurried in its direction. A fox-kit stared at Soren, his paws clutching the chain-links.

"Hey mister," he asked. "Are you a fox?"

"I am!" Soren said. "Why do you ask?"

"How come you got antlers?"

Soren smiled.

"Not everyone is born the same way," Soren replied. His enthusiasm bored the boy immediately, and he turned to chase his friends.

Soren smiled to himself and adjusted the strap that held the antlers on his head.

ৠ   ৠ   ৠ

Soren arrived as the foxes were holding an unannounced fox-only town hall meeting to determine new taxes on the use of antlers. The antler tax would be a way to constrain antler usage while ensuring that those who needed them most would get them. They agreed that those who were foxes were to be allocated one antler from all animals[1] who had two. This way, nobody would be overburdened by an abundance or lack of antler.

Soren was a clever fellow, but prone to intellectualizing his problems. He could rarely distinguish his world from an analytical treatise of his world, and so even his imagined antlers became abstracted into a head-pounding anxiety. His orange-

---

[1] *"Animal" descends from the Latin word "anima," the varied meanings of which include "breath" "life" "soul" and "mind." Harriet Ritvo, "Animal Consciousness: Some Historical Perspective."*

red tail twitched with the flicker of a doomed campfire.

Soren, the only fox at the antler meeting with branches strapped to his ears, had none to spare, and so he began a thorough interior study. Though these antlers were not naturally his, he wanted to be considered an animal who truly had them. Under the definitions laid out in this new legal definition of antlers under fox law, proving he had two *real* antlers required him to sacrifice one.

The absence of one antler, he figured, would amplify the realness of the one he'd keep. He was uneasy about the whole thing anyway. Solidarity would help him pass for a two-antlered beast, but what he really wanted was two antlers.

The solution, then, was to boldly embrace the missing and abstract antler. That is what an animal with two antlers would do. He stood up on a table, yelling "Aye!" and cracked the branch off his right ear.

"I shall blaze this path, gentlemen!"

The Fox Council made a raucous barking sound and took his antler first for redistribution. When Soren left, they threw the donated antler into a pile of confiscated raccoon treasure they'd deemed to be contraband. A few foxes hung out and chatted over beer.

There was no need to rejoice. It wasn't like that. They just felt Soren was a bit too wrapped up in the antler thing. The real experiment would be a few weeks later, when nobody acknowledged that no other antlers had been confiscated, and that the whole council meeting had been called strictly to get a rise out of Soren. As time wore on and Soren asked around, all the Fox Council members agreed to just pretend he'd only ever had the one antler all along.

৵   ৵   ৵

Sophie also dreamed of antlers. Long ago she was surrounded by deer like herself. In her memories, velvet streaks of lightning emerged from every surface. This city had none, as all the other antlered creatures had wandered away on isolated paths long ago. Sophie settled for the company of horses.

Sophie trotted home, hungover on the Palomino nightcaps, eyes peeled for foxes. She found her bedding between some trees and curled her four legs inward to rest. The trees have antlers too, she thought. Sometimes she missed the sight of antlers so much that she forgot the name for branches.

Instead of twisty bones, foxes wore an air of aloof sophistication on their foreheads. They don't tear you up with teeth anymore, these days. They stare at you with judgmental faces, but talk to you like friends.

৵   ৵   ৵

Soren marched, emboldened, through his day. Each conversation tested his ability to casually mention that he didn't mind sacrificing an antler for the benefit of others, that he was lucky enough to be born with two and had no concern about sacrificing one to help those born with none.

Sophie.

As the Fox Council had expected, it took about a week for Soren to begin questioning what was going on with the antler redistribution scheme, and another week before he could muster up the courage to make any kind of inquiry. It was inspired by an encounter with the city's only other antlered resident.

Sophie had woken up to the sight of a fox in the dark, standing and staring with a single branch tied to his ear. She tensed up, then remembered the common truce since the humans left. Her instinct reminded her of his instinct, and she tensed up again, on purpose.

"I'm sorry," said Soren. "I didn't mean to wake you."

"What do you want? Why are you watching me sleep?"

"It's just that I have a question," Soren stammered. "Don't laugh."

Sophie stared.

"Has anyone spoken to you about your antlers?" Soren asked. "Has anyone... asked to take one of them?"

"What? Why? Who?" Sophie replied. "What are you saying? Is this a fox riddle? Why would anyone want my antlers?"

"Antler," Soren corrected her. "Just the one. There's a law that's passed."

"A law? About antlers?"

"Just the one," Soren repeated. "To each who needs, an antler. From each who has, an antler."

"I've not heard that."

"It's Fox Law."

"Well luckily, I'm no fox, I'm deer. And deer don't follow Fox Law."

"No, but you know, the Fox Council has popular support across the Phylums."

"Yes, I know, but Fox Law isn't applicable to the rest of us. You don't follow Elk or Wolf Law?"

"God no. I mean, elk, OK. But..."

"Right. What if we all followed Wolf Law?"

Soren looked sullen.

"I had two antlers, and they took one."

Sophie began to question him but stopped.

"That's quite sad," she said. "I'm not sure I'd feel like myself without my antlers."

"Yes," said Soren. "But to surrender the antler, it was Fox Law. 'All antlered animals.' But I suppose

I was the only fox that had them. So, the law was really written just to take my antler."

"Well," Sophie offered, "'To each who needs, an antler,' right? Perhaps if you're the only fox who has given an antler, you're now the only fox who needs one." Soren perked up.

"That's very good of you!" he said. "I am officially in your debt."

Sophie knew that foxes could be real sons of bitches until they owed you a favor. Then they transformed into impressively loyal friends. To have stumbled into the good fortune of accidentally doing a favor for a fox, who are usually not so vulnerable as Soren, was a golden chance to make a much-needed friend.

"I accept your debt, Mr...?"

"Call me Soren."

"Sophie."

"Soren. It's Soren."

"I'm Sophie."

"Oh, you're Sophie, oh yes, OK. Nice to meet you. Let me know if you ever need a friend or favor." With a bow, Soren sprinted off to his burrow, to rest ahead of his big confrontation with the Fox Council.

~ ~ ~

Foxes, always inclined to claim residence in abandoned houses, were the first to enter the post-human city. The dogs had fled, turned feral and allied with wolves. The foxes took over the abandoned Victorians and revitalized empty neighborhoods. Foxes were the best organized of the new residents, which gave them significant sway over how the city was run, but no outright control over the other occupant Phylums.

Peter, the Fox Councilor, had no idea what antler law Soren was talking about.

"You've only ever had one of those damn tree things tied to your face," he told Soren. "I'm not sure what you're on about."

"We voted on a Fox Law addendum about two weeks ago, applied to all the animals with antlers, and I volunteered my antler to you and it was all a trick and I want it back."

"You only ever had one, Soren, but let's say you had more, they'd have been redistributed, right? Who knows who got your so-called antler. It could be on any damn thing."

"So, you admit I had one?"

"No. I'm just trying to reason with you. You're being very unreasonable, Soren. You're coming to me with some cockamamie story about having antlers on your head and then telling me we stole them in some sort of vote that never happened and would have been totally illegal if it had."

"It was legal for foxes," Soren started. "But I was the only fox who had them. And now I am the only fox who needs them."

At that moment, Roger, another Fox Council member, entered the room with a tree branch tied to his head.

"Roger!" Soren shouted. "You got my antler!"

"What are you talking about?" asked Roger.

"My antler, you have it. What luck!"

"I haven't got any antlers."

"Antler. Just the one. On your head."

"I don't see anything," said Peter.

"There's nothing on my head."

"Please, Roger. It's useless to you, but it's a terrible loss for me."

"This is old fox magic, Soren, and I'm disappointed. I'll not make any deals with you and your trickster ways just so you can get some antler thing that doesn't exist. We foxes have matured past that. Our social fabric requires the end of this kind of trickery. You don't want us to descend into Wolf Law, do you?"

Soren left in frustration and told his story to the bartender.

"Are you sure he had your antler on his head, Soren? I mean, you're known to see things sometimes."

"I saw it in bright light," said Soren. "I'm not crazy."

"You imagine things is all, you get excited. We all know you, Soren. Trust us when we say that Roger hasn't been going around with antlers."

"Just the one," Soren corrected him.

"As if that makes more sense!" the bartender yelled, exasperated.

"Honestly," said Soren, "I don't even know myself anymore. Perhaps if everyone else tells me it wasn't there, I've gone a little off? If so that's really worrying."

"Maybe so," the bartender said. "But don't worry about it. You're probably just stressed out about all the work you've got to do for me, but we can stretch out the repayment period a bit if you need to."

"What? What are you talking about?"

"You promised me you'd get me some more Wolf Mead. So far, nothing."

"Wolf Mead? I never promised anything about Wolf Mead."

"Soren, really? You're telling me that there's some crazy conspiracy to steal antlers, then you're telling me Roger has antlers, and now you're telling me I'm making up the deal with the Wolf Mead? Go back to your hole and bring back my bag of cash, then. Unless you've already spent it."

Soren got a bit self-conscious.

"No, no, I'm sorry, I've just forgotten. I'll sort it out. Thanks for the extension, I apologize. I've just been a bit stressed, I guess."

Soren went back to his burrow and found a burlap bag with a dollar sign painted on it. He peered in and saw a pile of sticks and leaves. He supposed it was actually cash, though, and started making schemes to get Wolf Mead. Nothing he saw made any sense, but he'd made a promise, and keeping that promise seemed like the one thing he could do to distinguish himself from crazy.

2. AN HONEST FOX

The problem, when you live in the city but leave it, is that you lose track of how many things you can still talk to. The old Victorian homes lost their spirit when the people and the cats went away. You can't talk to a staircase, but you can talk to the ivy winding its way around the railing. You can talk to a stone, but not the pulverized concrete of the sidewalk.

Built things were infused with the spirit of their makers. Human makers never thought to ask the things they'd built any questions at all. When the humans departed, they took these voices – voices they never listened to – and they could never speak again.

In the forest, Soren forgot that he could ask the night a question. The night in the city was always interrupted by the empty drone of streetlamps, which burned but had nothing to say. Street light was just a gossip, promising silence but revealing all the secrets.

Had Soren thought to ask the night, it may have shared advice on the forest that he'd forgotten in his city-dwelling. For example, a reminder that wolves have a special relationship with the mountains. Wolves protect the mountain from those who don't know them. Which complicates everything, because it means you must know the mountains, but also know the wolves. Mountains were simple. Wolf Law was anarchic.

Soren may have also asked the fog, or the dew, or the flowers the dew slept on. But alone in the dark, Soren began to think instead, as he often did. While examining the bag of cash from the bartending badger, Soren had resolutely determined that it was a bag of sticks and leaves. He nonetheless had high hopes that returning to the Fox Council with a supply of Wolf Mead would earn him some goodwill and restore his reputation amongst his colleagues. He'd take good cheer and trade it for a leg up on getting the antler thing sorted.

He lit a fire in a lantern and wandered into the forest. He liked wolves *alright*, and they were probably reasonable when it came to trade. He brought the bag of twigs and leaves and figured he could use a bit of old fox magic to his advantage. It was a change of moral position for him, but he'd decided he could compromise.

Sophie had been melancholy, and so she wrote a letter to the stone with antlers whom she had loved and once tried desperately to keep from sliding into the sea.

Dear _____,

What is there to say about the water on my fur? It always feels more like slime than salt. The sea is a bath for you, softening your corners, polishing you up, wrapping you in a blanket. I preferred the solid stone beneath my hooves. And then I watched as the glaciers came and move you. Trails behind you, a wake of sand, and then you reached the sea. You could have formed rivers if you'd taken your time. But you didn't.

You paused more than you moved. You stood still in miniscule increments until you got there. It passed in minutes. I stood in front of you the whole time, just as I always had, as if I could kill the conspiracy between time and a spinning glowing core of the planet. What good are my antlers if they can't stop the pressures of a planet and the passage of time? That was all I was asked to do.

When you pushed me to the sea I had to get out from ahead. I realized you were working against me. I realized you had wanted to go there to be swallowed. And so I let you go, lest you drown me, too. But I miss you every day.

Yours,
Sophie.

  ✿ ✿ ✿

Sophie wanted to deliver the letter. She could have gone to the stone in the sea, but she knew the Deerstone's true spirit lived within the mountain. They had pushed each other so hard that the stone's hooves had transformed into black streaks of keratin scraped across slate.[2]

Sophie, head down, resisted with all her body. The stone drifted toward the sea, relentless and unyielding.

Wander into the trees sometime. The forest has a way of taking the unknowable mist and whispers within you and showing you a spider web. Then you'll say, "Aha! A spider web! It's a spider web strung up between my ribs! My spirit is crafted of fragile silks!" Then you write it down and it becomes the way you know yourself. Later you meet the monkeyflower and the dew hangs off its lip. "Aha!" you say. "There it is, that precarious sense of being just about to let go."

Sophie went to the forest to deliver her letter. She remembered the trees and sound of the voice spoken by the night, she recalled the sarcastic tone of the Shrubby Butterweed's so-called "jokes." But tonight, she was silent, and the forest did not offer her its typical translations.

No spirit of a flower or a spiderweb, of the dew or of the monkeyflower, was up to translating

---

[2] Douglas H. Chadwick, a field biologist, described the function of hooves to stop friction in his 2002 book about Mountain Goats, "A Beast the Color of Winter," p. 52: "This is not a fancy way of restating the effect of distributing and balancing the grip I just described. What is going on here is a fanning out of forces. If all the downward force could be converted into opposing sideways forces, it would in effect be cancelled out. If you stand in a narrow hallway, place your hands on the opposite walls, and push as hard as you can against them you can very nearly hold your weight off the ground. With the mountain goat's foot, we are only talking about one two-toed hoof and only a partial sideways component of forces, but the result is the same to a degree: Friction and more friction."

Sophie's sorry state.[3] She wasn't asking. Her inner mist and whispers were full of wait. Time distills that waiting into droplets. Sophie knew the dewdrops within her would never touch the droplets suspended from the redwoods or the monkeyflower's lips. The precipitation within her was an isolated ecosystem. That was the broken nature of who she was.[4]

She often sensed other spirits were more malleable, that other flesh was permeable. But she was not. She was distinct, tragically complete within herself, formed by some missing thing that was unnamed, not even through the talented translation machines of moss and seafoam. Her innerspace was unmetaphorable. The forest was simply forest.

She arrived at the space where she had met the stone with antlers – it was still a deer then. Now she was meeting the absence of that stone, a just-as-heavy hole. Sophie stomped her hoof, twice, to gather the attention of the local spirits, and then bowed to show them she was friendly.

---

[3] *"The problem of how environment and feelings are related comes to a head with the question, can a sense of spaciousness be associated with the forest? From one viewpoint, the forest is a cluttered environment, the antithesis of open space. Distant views are nonexistent. ... The forest, no less than the bare plain, is a trackless region of possibility. Trees that clutter up space from one viewpoint are, from another, the means by which a special awareness of space is created, for the trees stand one behind the other as far as the eyes can see, and they encourage the mind to extrapolate to infinity. The open plain, however large, comes visibly to an end at the horizon. The forest, although it may be small, appears boundless." Tuan, Yi-Fu. Space and Place: The Perspective of Experience. Minneapolis: U Minnesota P, 1977. (56)*

4 *"How I have felt the shape that parting takes. How I see it still: A dark invincible cruel something that holds out a fragile unity and offers it and tears it straight in two." Rainer Maria Rilke, Pg 167.*

She placed the letter on the edge of the precipice. She felt unresolved. She knew she was bowing to the spirit of the absent thing, but she wasn't yet ready to say goodbye to that lover of hers that had turned, through sheer stubborn force of will, into a sinking stone out by the sea cliff.

As the fog came in, covering all the absences and presences in the same dense cloak, she decided she would not go to the stone at all, not yet. Maybe she would go away instead: a vacation.

And in her wandering through the forest to her home, she spotted a fox in the distance, nibbling on tofu triangles, a single branch tied to his ear.

ର ର ର

Soren wandered between birch trees and the fog rolled in. The thickness convinced him he'd get no further, and he gave up hope that he would rouse the wolves tonight. He stopped upon a fallen tree and unpacked a triangle made of fried tofu from his pouch. He contemplated as he nibbled.

A crunchy sound tore through the chew. He stopped his mouth as his ears twitched: The brittle sound of a cracking leaf. All he saw was moonlight bouncing off the metallic-tasting haze rolling in off the sea.

"Who's there?" he called. The answer came in the suddenly silenced sound of the leaf crunch. "I'm harmless," he said, cringing just in time not to stammer in the statement. He'd announced he was easy prey, loud and clear.

"I'm Soren," he said. "I'm a fox."

"Soren?" came the reply, then a short trotting over the leaves.

"Oh!" said Soren. Antlers emerged from the tightly-wound mist. "Sophie!"

They exchanged remarks about how odd it was to find one another in the middle of the birch trees. Sophie demurred from telling her reasons. Soren took the opportunity to expound on his, bringing her up to the now of it, where just as he'd given up on finding wolves he'd found a friend instead. Then he caught himself.

"How... How do I know you're really you?" he asked her. "It's a bit on-the-nose, don't you think? With all these other fox magics running around my head, you can't blame me for asking."

Sophie shrugged.

"Do you want me to go?" she asked. Soren decided that the best way to gather information about potential trickery was to go along with it and hope the scheme would reveal itself along the way. He'd lull her into a false sense of security and hope she got sloppy.

"No," he said.

They agreed they couldn't get anywhere that night and that they should have a sleep. They shared conversation in whispers just because it was nice.

"I lived here before," she said. "For a long time. Coyotes used to be here, then they started going around, into the city, up over the bridge. Are coyotes part of the Wolf Union now?"

"Yes," said Soren. He wondered if that answer would reveal too much, but thought better. Foxes knew fox history. "Foxes are the only holdouts."

"This place was just us, the coyotes and raccoons. After the departure the other deer just sort of wandered out to do their own thing, while raccoons moved into the boats. I thought the coyotes stayed here."

"Yes," said Soren. "This bit of forest at the end of the bridge is the spot the wolves come in to trade. They don't go beyond the old gates around this forest. I know the bartender comes here to get Wolf Mead, but I suppose it's a matter of luck to find them."

Soren assumed the bridge story was part of the ruse. He waited for Sophie to fall asleep and then he stared up and over, looking for the telltale fox tail that would blow her cover. Indeed, he found one. Soren was briefly enraged. Then he engaged in his favorite pastime: second guessing himself. Do deer naturally have tails, he wondered? Or do they have that fuzzy rump with the furry flower above the butt? Soren fretted. This all felt like a fox plot, but he couldn't remember elk from white tails and he'd hate to come across as someone who couldn't tell the difference. He also hated to make an accusation against a friend he'd promised a favor to.

Soren had long ago decided that the shock of finding out he'd been lied to was far less painful than living his life in a state of perpetual mistrust. It made him easy prey. He decided to solve the problem by going to sleep.

As the light began to stream through dewy mist, Soren woke first. He hadn't noticed, the night before, that he'd gone to sleep beside a magnificent tree. It was tall and wide, with strong bark.

The Tree.

Soren looked again at Sophie, and let her sleep. Her tail was golden brown, but long. She was a fox trying to trick him, he decided. Most good things were. He went for a wander, thinking he'd make an escape. He walked around the tree, and then leaned over, groping around for a stone. He found a shard of one, and heaved it up upon his chest. It was all his front paws could hold, and he contemplated its weight. He walked over to Sophie, held the stone high above his head, and dropped it onto her leg. She stammered up, but the leg was unable to bend correctly, and she fell to the ground.

"What are you doing?" she called out.

"Show me what you are!" he cried.

"I'm Sophie! What are you doing?" she seemed pitiful, and the sight of Sophie's leg bent backward was such a heartbreaking betrayal of her natural form that he knew then and there that it was a fox trick. He lifted the stone and dropped it again on her leg. She barked a horrible, guttural sound, losing the dignity of her chosen voice. The pain, he could tell, was overwhelming her. He could stop now, but she hadn't yet revealed her fox spirit.

"You have a fox tail," he said, calmly. "I don't like this, but you've got to tell the truth. I can't..." he stopped, and looked at the situation, and he grew enraged at the state of things. He just wanted certainty again, and he had committed to uncovering the certainty beneath the layers of tricks he'd been embroiled in. He lifted the rock again over his head, and in a surge of power in his arms, he tossed it down again, this time upon her antler. It cracked easily. He took the antler in his hand, found its sharpest piece, and held it to her chest.

Her chest resisted the plunging of the sharp end of the antler at first, but he pushed it further until it broke open and accepted it. Sophie began to choke out a deep crimson blood. It came out from her nose; she couldn't breathe or speak.

Soren realized he'd made the wrong decision when she didn't revert, then, to a fox form. His own blood, still contained within him, rushed from his face to his lower paws. Regret boiled his insides. He choked on the reality of what he had done and the loss of any sense of himself that he had once understood. He was damaged and unable to be repaired. He fell to the ground, and cried terrible tears as Sophie wheezed through spattered blood.

From behind the birch trees emerged the individual members of the fox council, cheering.

"Well done, Soren! You fell for the old fox magic after all," said Peter Fox. "It was easy, once we got you paranoid about us. We didn't have to do anything after that. You were the only fox dumb enough to trick himself into a horrible mess!"

The foxes erupted into cheering barks of laughter. Then the sun became piercing, and the dew dissolved from the air, drying away with Soren's sweat. The fox council stopped, looking skyward. Through the piercing light: a white fox, winged, with a satchel and a sword. They all knew what it meant. The light brightened, and everything went the opposite of blind. The winged fox told him something.

He jolted upright, howling. He looked around. Sophie was beside him, upright, still and silent, staring. There was the magnificent tree, tall and wide, with strong bark. It wore a twisted rope around itself, the mark of a revered figure among the unspeaking flora.

Soren looked again at Sophie. Her tail was short and golden-brown. She cast the shadow of a deer, not a fox.

"Oh no," he said. "Oh no! I had the most horrible dream," he said. "I did the most terrible thing. I've revealed myself to be a monster."

Sophie couldn't move. Her response took some time to reverse.

"Please, please don't be frightened," Soren said. "Or maybe you should be frightened. I'm afraid I don't know myself at all."

After some time, Sophie relaxed again. Soren had been quiet, looking at the tree.

"Do you know this tree?" he asked her.

"Hello," she said. Soren stiffened. He'd forgotten that the tree might be watching them.

"   ," said the tree.

When trees of a certain power speak, there's no sound. They have no mouth or lungs to vibrate any air, no throat for vibrations to echo through. The way you hear a tree is to hear the tree by knowing. That's all there was to it.

City foxes had mostly lost that language. It was a rusty skillset, and many had already forgotten how to hear the wood or the vine or petalstems resonate inside them with reaffirming certainty. Trees in particular. They spoke so quickly, because you already knew what they would say if you understood how to listen to them say it.

Soren understood the tree like a half-learned foreign language. When it spoke, meanings came fleetingly, and were overwhelmed. It reminded Soren of conversations with a friend by the sea. He heard her only when the waves receded, and lost her voice whenever they returned.

ॐ   ॐ   ॐ

The two decided to advance to the bridge to search for wolves.

The bridge was the orange-red color that becomes sacred against blue skies. Many days it is protected by the ocean mist, and other days it is protected by the coyote faction of the Wolf Union. Few ever crossed it, because few ever bothered to leave the city. The other side was lush and green hills and a small town of boats that the raccoons had taken over, but they'd come to the north of the city and deliver fish in trade for shiny silver things.

If the Wolf Union had fully retreated to the other side of the bridge, it would be strange to do so without notice to the other Phylums. This concerned Sophie, who understood wolf logic a bit better than Soren, who became anxious even at the idea of understanding his Canidae cousins.[5]

The sun reflected on the rising red towers of the sacred bridge, high above the cottony mist. The trumpet blats rang out at steady intervals, signifying the presence of mist and not coyotes.

Even at the entrance, they were greeted only by a handful of squirrels and butterflies, who never paid attention to the comings and goings of dogs or foxes.

It was Sophie who suggested they go over the bridge. She had craved some adventuring to find some place that hadn't been saturated by a thick

---

[5] *"It is always possible to bind together a considerable number of people in love, so long as there are other people left over to receive the manifestations of their aggressiveness. I once discussed the phenomenon that is precisely communities with adjoining territories, and related to each other in other ways as well, who are engaged in constant feuds and in ridiculing each other. I gave this phenomenon the name of "the narcissism of minor differences"... We can now see that it is a convenient and relatively harmless satisfaction of the inclination to aggression, by means of which cohesion between the members of the community is made easier." Sigmund Freud, Civilization and its Discontents, trans. and ed., James Strachey (New York: W. W. Norton, 1961), pp. 58-63.*

residue of longing and memory. She left that part out in her exaltations to Soren, focused instead on the prospect of adventure, and the means with which such a mission would help him.

Soren was reluctant, though the adventure was mostly to his own benefit. It was quite a convenient coincidence to have a friend along on the errand. He knew it was the best chance of getting Wolf Mead, and Sophie was better company than he'd find on a chartered racoon fishing boat.

Some of his dream had lingered over Sophie, and he was uneasy about trusting himself not to fall into paranoid bewitchment. Perhaps some time away from foxes would do him some good.

As he let himself imagine time away from the Fox Council, he had another thought, which he had not prepared for, which is that the Fox Council really were a miserable bunch of shits. He would get the Wolf Mead, sure, but he felt himself grow a bit more solid in himself. He could use the mead to demand not only that his antler be returned, but to have a higher position among the Councilors, or he'd put that stupid fucking badger bartender out of business. Anger, though, was unbecoming a fox, so he quickly shook off his feelings.

"An adventure would be good for us both," he said.

      ✌   ✌   ✌

The pair cut a pathway through thick mist that obscured even their view of each other. The towers could be seen, from time to time, but straight ahead, they may as well have been blindfolded in fresh linens.

They crossed slowly and frequently lost each other. Sophie was naturally fast, and Soren, a flaneur, was the more cautious and ambling one. The sound of hoof on steel let Soren know where Sophie was, and there was only the narrow path to follow.

One step in front of another in low visibility triggered some boredom in Soren, and boredom triggered rumination. He contemplated his newfound independence, and his discovery of the need to trust himself, and began to wonder how, exactly, that begins to happen. It's easy enough to stand up to specters in imagined conversations, he thought, but would he be able to do so when face to face with a real predicament? He hadn't yet been tested. In fact, he had carried out a murder in his dreams, a murder based entirely on fox tricks.

Soren's introspection was interrupted by the howl of coyotes. The clatter of hoof on steel stopped. A moment passed, and the fog blasted its trumpet.

Soren was surprised he recognized it. Fox Council and the Wolf Union had an awkward and uneasy friendship. There was a lingering suspicion among the Wolf Union (which contained all wild dogs) that foxes simply thought they were too good for the rest of them. Foxes were the first into the city while all other dogs fled. Foxes were a well-mannered and sophisticated species that held themselves aloof from dogs, though they were as much a part of the family as a Corgi, a Coyote, or a Jackal.

It helped, though, that foxes hunted through trickery and illusions, and that they had obtained special magics that helped them get by. The Wolf Union tended to cut through these deceptions with some extreme forms of justice. Foxes suspected of deception, or anything suspected of being a fox in secret, could be torn apart by the teeth of the pack. For wolves, this had proven an effective means of disillusionment and reduced incidents of foxes taking on alluring forms to trick them out of services or food. Among the urbanized fox elite, wolves had a menacing presence. Violence was rare, but always possible, and just the threat was enough to keep foxes in line whenever they ventured beyond city limits, which eventually became never.

When Soren cleared the fog, he could see Sophie frozen in the center of a circle of wild dogs. The howling had started and there was nowhere for her to go. Soren barked in the primal language understood by all Canidae. The wolves, not recognizing Soren's right to speak, turned, distracted, and howled in unison.

Soren was shaking with nerves, but angry and frightened, which triggered in him the highest wail he could muster, a sound deeper than his lungs. It carried over at the precise moment of the fog trumpet, and the wolves, hearing it all at such a higher register, cringed. They backed away. There was a hierarchy among the Wolf Union: The pitch of the bark instinctively rose alongside the intensity of feeling; to give respect to sharpest howl was a matter of dignity. When the wolves came together they would come to consensus, howling all night until the deepest feeling had been found.

Sophie, however, was not privy to this understanding. Inside of her body an electric wire had snapped, triggering the muscles of absolute, mindless panic. She began running, swinging her antlers about as she leaped and stomped in a frenzy designed to maim whatever dared approach her. The sparks triggered her back legs, which the pack retreated from, but also the front, which sent the wolves running in their own panicked circles around her.

Internally, she was present, but her thoughts weren't spared from the spiraling panic, either. The panic might stop for a split second, and Sophie's consciousness would emerge from it, only to itself be swept aside, as if gored by her own antlers. She had the sense of watching herself move until an internal scream tore through her internal monologue: RUN, RUN, RUN.

And so she did, in the only direction that seemed to her like an exit. To the right, into a wall of fog, and then a sensation of flight.

ৎ৶   ৎ৶   ৎ৶

Soren kept his focus on the subject at hand: calming an angry pack of wild dogs. He decided the best approach was the simplest fox magic: charm.

"Calm down, everyone!" Soren shouted. "What's all this fuss about? I'd just like to cross the bridge, if I may."

The dogs stopped howling one by one. A small coyote emerged from the pack.

"You can't cross this bridge," he said. "You've got to pay a toll. We don't want you spreading. You have no idea how to live on the other side."

"What's the toll?" Soren asked. He had the hunch that the wolves were improvising.

Indeed, they all howled. Clearly this was their first go at the toll thing.

"What's in the bag?" A small wolf gestured at Soren's burlap sack. Soren contemplated for a moment.

"Sticks and leaves," he told them. "I'm trying to trade them for Wolf Mead."

"Why would we trade our Mead for sticks and leaves?" the small wolf asked.

"I don't know, but it often seems to work. The badger in the city always does it. He told me to come out here and do it for him."

"You're lying," snarled the wolf.

"No. Here, have a look..." Soren opened the bag, exposing gold coins and stacks of cash.

"What kind of idiot prank is this?" asked the wolf. "If that's sticks and leaves, it's enough to get you across the bridge. Give it to us."

"I'm afraid you're mistaken," said Soren. "It's just an old fox trick. You're enchanted."

The wolves went into howls of laughter.

"You're a piss-poor practitioner of fox magic, then, if you're trying to convince us that what we're seeing isn't gold. What's your endgame?"

"I want you to trust me," said Soren. "I want you to know that I don't tell lies."

"You only lie for Wolf Mead, then?" asked a voice from the back.

"Yes!" another wolf cried. "You just said you'd trade this bag for Wolf Mead. You admit you're a swindle!"

"No," said Soren. "I told you the truth, and I'd tell it to the Wolf Meader. Just as I hope you'd let me through, I'd hoped I could make a trade. The real currency, you see," — Soren had just realized this for himself — "Is an honest fox."[6]

3. JUG JAM AT RACCOON GROTTO

I always thought of you at the intersection of Fillmore and Broadway. As you come up Fillmore from the Pagoda you can see the edge of the street as if it is about to fall into an abyss. After crossing Fillmore up into Broadway, the entire bay and the coast roll out in front of you, the palace, the prison, the sea.

Every time, I think: I can see everything but you. I want to show you how beautiful it can be as you get close to the edge, how smoothly it seems you can glide down there, into the sea, without crashing.

But maybe I am meant for crashing.[7] This is my way: To throw myself into fear and endless longing. To find the most vulnerable bits and print them, in my own handwriting, exposing myself.

The pleasure of love (I don't dare call this a joy) may come from the feeling of jumping into the rushing water of futility, the futility of trying to become another person, and getting carried away by

---

[7] *"The inalienable boundary between two people, and recognizing the futility of trying to eliminate it." - Adorno*

the rush. The leap seemed so exciting, tumultuous. But now I am more excited by the discovery of my own islands. Why abandon everything, if there is something to seek out, some beach to land on?

The cold water purifies things somehow. Giving everything up for the leap, though, means we die. Or end up somewhere else, bruised and covered in kelp.[8] *I would do it all to have you here, always, but ultimately, you are always there, somewhere beyond my skull, my body, my fur. I don't know how to have you any closer, it's impossible. I am only ever dreaming of you, even if your stomach rises and falls beside mine.*[9] *So why do I miss you even when the dream is always here, and was all I ever had of you?*

Yours,
Sophie

ও   ও   ও

Sophie awoke, having written and delivered a letter in her dreams. She found herself suspended 212 feet above a roiling sea. She tried to look around, but her head was stuck. The sea surrounded her vision like a dome. She couldn't move; her muscles tensed, but found no traction.

Surely, she hadn't died. Or perhaps she had, and this was some aftermath of death, some in-between

---

[8] *"On top of all else, the unhappy lover has to admit that, exactly where he thought he was forgetting himself, he loved himself only."* -Adorno.

[9] *"Clarity is your stomach against my spine."* - Maria Teutsch

state between worlds. Maybe, she thought, excitedly, she had merged with the spirit of the fog?

Then she saw the squirrel. Squirrels had done as much as they could to withdraw from the other creatures and preserve their domain of languagelessness. They spoke among themselves only to reaffirm an annual vow of silence. They hoped, with enough time ruled by disuse, they'd forget language altogether.

When the animal truces were negotiated, squirrels had lost their predators, and with it, their interest in what anyone else was getting up to. They'd developed a reputation for a specific daftness and were usually muttered about as "idiot squirrels."

It didn't help that squirrels frequently did the same shit that drove humans crazy. They'd chew holes in wires, steal food, break things without explaining themselves. Seeing the idiot accelerated Sophie's panic as the squirrel scurried off and transformed into a disembodied gnawing sound.

Sophie at once understood that she was trapped in a net beneath the bridge, and that the idiot squirrel was chewing on the netting. A malevolent squirrel would at least be killing her from some malicious purpose. An idiot, though, what could you do? Just shout no as it chewed through one wire and promptly moved to another.

The squirrel reappeared and stood still, breathing in a nervous pulse. It twitched, and Sophie tensed. The squirrel bit down on the last bit of net.

Sophie was in a momentary free-fall broken by a sharp tug and swing. Her body crashed against steel. The entanglement of hoof and wire sent a sharp pain through her leg. The sea spun in circles around her, but did not come any closer.

Her eyes met a steel vermillion bridge and a wall of rushing sea. The squirrel scurried ahead. Limping down a spiral staircase, Sophie came out to a concrete island and contemplated a swim. The fog was rolling in, and the trumpets sounded in deep, familiar tones. In the distance, a yellow light pierced the dusk, coming closer and closer: a raccoon ship.

So this was "adventure," Sophie thought.

∾ ∾ ∾

The Eldest Raccoon.

The water felt cold on the paws of the Eldest Raccoon as he massaged the clamshells beneath the stream. It wasn't so necessary to eat clams clean, but he'd take any excuse for the tickling of his fingers.

The Eldest Raccoon lost himself in his hands, in gratitude to the beings within the shells he was about to break. Then he stood still in sensation with an empty mind.

A rustling sound snapped him back, a robin slipping from its perch into the sky. The Eldest Raccoon contemplated the interrupted silence with the language that had flooded back.

The kits had no sense of this silence. They only knew *this* world, the one the humans had left for their inheritance. He would be the last to know the world before the cool silence running over paw pads was interrupted by the meanings of words that had been assigned to it. He would be the last to know the non-word for clamshell, paw-pad, rushing-stream moments, one infinite word that could never be transcribed.

He sat still again in silence, and might have wept, but instead slipped past tears (themselves born from meaning) and returned to a silence that would, inevitably, break.

It was the red fur of a fox emerging from the sacred bridge that did it.

ॐ　ॐ　ॐ

Soren had found his way to the bohemian Raccoon Grotto on the other side of the bridge.

Raccoons took quickly to the nautical life. Remote but accessible, the town had become a refuge not just for its steady supply of Wolf Mead, Pinecone Wine, and Acorn Cocktails, but also for a sloppy form of raccoon jazz performed with jugs, banjos, fishing buckets, clam shells slapped on sticks, and rubber bands strapped across oyster shells.

Soren laid to rest in front of the jug jam. A crowd of drunken furry creatures gathered, lured by music, but also the ceremonial shaking of the shiny things; a reflective collection of polished stones and metals strung to sticks and dangled before candlelight.

Raccoons had their own thing, thought Soren. He pondered what was the thing that foxes had. It was easier in relief.

Foxes weren't thieves, that was badgers.
Foxes weren't artsy, that was raccoons.
Foxes weren't wild, that was wolves.
Foxes weren't wise, that was trees.
Foxes weren't idiots, that was squirrels.
Foxes weren't poets, that was deer.

Foxes were a bit of all those things as well as none. They had their deceptions, which was a kind of art. Too few other creatures had magic, at least not the magic for illusions. Foxes had their lutes. They had smarts and cunning, though wisdom always seemed elusive.

Foxes had the freedom to pass as anything they chose. He'd never felt he quite "belonged" amongst foxes, but nothing else had ever made sense, either.

Soren let his mind come to a pause on the subject, and focused again on the jug-and-clam raccoon jam. A fat raccoon plucking rubber bands wrapped taut around an oyster shell. Soren wrote this down.

"A fat raccoon plucking rubber bands wrapped taut around an oyster shell."

It reminded him of his own wobble. He rose up, transformed into a gray beast with a black mask, and played along a bit with his lute. If his tail revealed his true form, nobody seemed to mind too much. Raccoons just weren't that way.

A few hours passed, and the raccoon cabaret split up a case full of baubles seven ways. One seventh of the take was enough to get Soren a night of fried tofu and a pint of sap milk as he planned his next moves. He placed it in his satchel and curled up by a log.

The night turned silent, save for the fog's trumpet and some distant raccoon revelry. His mind wandered to Sophie, whose spirit had become either the fog, or the sea, or the bridge. He may not know how to find her among either.

He shot up his head and made his way to the wood that reached into the water, among the fishing boats. Whether she had become fog or sea or bridge, he had all three in front of him. From the edge of the dock, wrapped in a mist, his feet tickled by sea foam, with awe for the vermillion towers, he let himself be the surface that absorbed them, made them firm and present and felt.

He clapped his hands. Then he clapped his hands, and bowed, and clapped; he clapped again, then bowed, then clapped. Clapped his hands, then bowed, then clapped.

Then clapped.

Then slept.

❧   ❧   ❧

The antlered stone was still a deer when Sophie met her. The Deerstone deer, back then, was standing, legs askew, in a crouched position poised to flee.

Sophie had understood her own center of gravity then, having earned it or simply not having lost it yet— she wasn't sure which. But if you surround yourself with wolves, you learn that they will howl to gather others at the sight of a terrified and trembling prey; they will howl a retreat at the sight of anything else.

It was hard to strike a position of fearlessness, even when you know the wolves have a legally binding agreement not to tear your body apart through various sets of gnashing teeth. The law is there because they want to, and would, unless something made up a reason not to. Those reasons were as flimsy as the Deerstone's deer-form legs.

Sophie was right to identify with the Deerstone doe. Both had a resemblance in form, if not in demeanor, down to the rare appearance of feminine antlers. Sophie, too, was unsure how to use them at first, but found them to be a blessing.

"If you stand," Sophie told the doe-formed Deerstone, "You should stand straight. If you lay on the ground, weigh yourself like a stone. This is your place, and you are right to be here. If they don't believe they can move you, they won't even try. They will move on to some hollow feathery thing, or something that looks off balance."

The doe shot up, out of self-consciousness, and seemed to ask if she was doing it right.

"I'm not your center of gravity," Sophie told her.

❧ ❧ ❧

Sophie's hoof slipped, and she wobbled, interrupting her nostalgia. She stomped and ducked on the rocking raccoon boat. The pilots were showing off tricks with the steering wheel, but the sea was choppy, and the fog was thick, and so it wasn't all that fun.

One steered with his feet, before a sideways wave knocked him down and spun the wheel. Another stuck the wheel with his bindle-stick and stopped the spin but then began to try to steer with just the wood pole.

Amidst the clamor, soundtracked by a drunken raccoon with a snakeskin banjo, Sophie collapsed into a pile of silver slips of light that had been pulled from the sea. She scrambled to stand. A drunken raccoon grabbed a small fish from the net and offered it to her.

"No, thank you," she said. "I'm a grass-eater."

The raccoon nodded knowingly, but then the bindle-pole snapped, and the waves tumbled the boat askew, spilling the sardines sideways over the surface of the ship. The fish slapped at air and paws and wooden floorboards, and Sophie collapsed again. She did not get up again until they reached the shore.

Sophie was not fond of the maritime tradition.

      ৰ   ৰ   ৰ

Soren's most immediate concerns about the future seemed easily set aside amidst the breezy atmosphere of the Raccoon Grotto. Perhaps just getting out of the city would be enough. Wasn't he really just seeking revenge?

Every storefront presented the illusion of a future. "I could work there," Soren thought as he wandered the Grotto. He said it about the tailor, the bar, the sardine stand, the hand-washing-station, the rope-and-knot, the tackle-and-bait, the kitnergarten, the fruit-and-nut, and the paw-feather club. Every career seemed a delightful respite from his career as a regulator of Fox Law.

With the sun up the city was mostly shuttered, and he was able to sustain the illusion uninterrupted. Dusk arrived, and the windows of the city creaked open to reveal the nightly living of the Grotto. Raccoons ran to and fro with bindle sticks, unpacked wooden carts to sell their corn and fresh-washed foodstuffs.

      ৰ   ৰ   ৰ

Sophie's boat crew had dropped her off at the Ferry Station in the morning, then unloaded their sardines and fell asleep. It was a week before they'd return to the Grotto, and Sophie thought it best not to dawdle.

Sophie knew the shortest path back required a wander through the Gray. It was the least habitable part of the city, invented by the humans before they departed. It was built from scraps of rubbish and debris, the legend went, and piled on top of the sea. They melted stones and sand into garbage mud, pouring it between more waste, transforming the sea into an Earth without soil. They poured tiny stones into molds and piled them until they blocked out the sky from every angle.

Sophie knew the place was some strange human thing, and though she had never met or seen a person, she assumed they had a reason for what they did, even if it was as incomprehensible to her as Bee Poetry. Humans built spaces the way bees wrote poems. Harsh and cold and sharp and dull, but reflective of some innate bee-rhythm or human-ness.

The music of this place was silent to her now. If there was ever a conversation between the humans and the steel and the crushed stone, she would never hear it. Everything has a spirit, but the things that are made have the spirit of their makers. When the humans disappeared, so did the spirit inside of their things. It was a silent, lonely place.

Only birds seemed OK with it, because they could dip in quickly and then fly above it. That left the Gray's surface as the only place a creature could wander in complete isolation, detached from the chorus of chatter between all the life that went on elsewhere.

Sophie entered the mouth of the place. Not even ten feet in and her hooves echoed. Surrounded by the emptiness of shade and silence, it felt impossible to ever be part of the sun again.

As she wandered deeper in, her mind played tricks on her: the wind, in a hurry to get out of there, kicked up some debris that she mistook for life. But the glance revealed another figure, out across the distant and repeating sameness: A tired, solitary tree, stained by a harsh sliver of light slowly rolling over the surface of its leaves. A hole had been allowed in the floor, just larger than its trunk, where rain could come into its roots. Another hole, several feet above, had been cut into the ceiling. But the sun was blocked by the steel and glass towers. Wherever its roots reached, they would be stymied by concrete and tar.

Sophie felt herself in agreement with the tree. The forest is a language of translation, a series of metaphors reflecting an internal world. In the place of silent or absent spirits, another language was spoken; the spirit that haunts the spaces between words. She looked at the tree.

"   ," she said.

"

," the tree replied.

It took three hours.

And then she forgot it. She knew she'd forgotten it, and could recall it, like chasing the contours of a dream from some stray image. When she finally surrendered the memory, she felt, for the first time, like maybe she understood these human things. She wondered if somehow, by understanding this concrete poem, she had inherited some human disease. She could stay here and study the language of the absent and the dead. Among all the shade and stone, it felt like the only true story. She resented her hunger and avoided it for days. She would have stayed perfectly alone and still forever. Instead, she had to forage, so she headed to high ground, imagining some layer of grass and flowers blooming in the sunlight above.

There were no plants, just a line of crows in queue to enter a building. Her approach triggered leaps and cackles. "Do you know where I could find something to eat?"

The crows said the only food around was inside the pigeon's cinema. Everything else was closed forever. If she got in line she could get some popcorn or something, but she'd have to buy a ticket.

Sophie ordered a popcorn and went to see the film. She had already forgotten the tree completely.

વ્   વ્   વ્

Crows sat on the backs of chairs, snacking on rodent carrion. Sophie curled up in an aisle as the light dimmed, and then on the screen, two giant figures appeared. They were humans. Sophie was stunned. Hadn't all the humans disappeared? She looked around at the crows, who didn't flinch.

The two humans were sitting at a cafe, eating breakfast. They were young. The man had red hair and the woman had large brown eyes. They were speaking about things Sophie didn't understand. Sophie wondered why they were ignoring the audience of animals, but then she remembered where she was. Humans must have always ignored animals. Then she realized: This is a play. How strange that the only humans she had ever seen would be part of a human performance!

The humans communicated, and the woman seemed to get angry. The man leaned back and looked upset at something he'd done. Then the woman left. Suddenly, the entire stage transformed into a window looking into a park frozen over by ice. Sophie had seen snow once, in the mountains, but not like that. It looked like the Gray. She wondered why people were so fascinated with things that weren't grass? But then she thought perhaps she was fascinated with grass simply because of who she was. A deer, she reasoned, probably values grass the way bees value yellow things. She congratulated herself on being so empathetic to other species, of understanding the differences between them.

A woman was running in the snow next to another woman and they were making some conversation. What were they running from? Maybe just for fun, Sophie thought. Then the people stopped, and a woman started crying hysterically. Maybe they weren't running for fun? The woman must be sad that they aren't running fast enough, or because it's cold outside, Sophie decided.

Sophie was sort of bored by looking at the same two or three people repeatedly, talking to one another in an incomprehensible language. Her attention turned to the crows. What were they getting out of this?

A few minutes later the crying woman met a new man in a very confined space. She showed no emotion at first, but he smiled while he spoke, and then they smiled at each other. Then she was with the woman friend again but this time she didn't cry. Things must be warmer there now, Sophie thought.

Indeed, the next thing she saw was a city, even bigger than theirs, with trees in bloom and the sun streaming over a bridge. The man was running to various bakeries and people kept shaking their heads at him. Finally, she found a strange, flakey pastry that Sophie had never seen before. A woman put it in a bag for him and he went to a park to meet the woman.

The camera focused on the bag and then Sophie saw the man and the woman talking and the man smiled and said something that made the woman very happy, and then when he turned around, presumably to grab the bag, A CROW HAD GOTTEN INTO

THE BAG AND WAS TEARING UP THE PASTRY.

The crows in the audience went full-throttle in their cawing. Some started flying around the theater. The man on the screen turned and looked very upset and tried to scare the crow on the screen away as the woman laughed. Many crows in the theater started flying at the screen, biting the man, but the man focused only on the crow that had eaten his baklava.

Then the scene moved on to the two people in a restaurant. The crows started to leave. The film stopped and the lights in the theater came up.

"Isn't there more to see?" Sophie asked. The crows said it was all boring after that part and that they had other things to do. There were other theaters, though, and maybe if she paid a bit extra, the pigeons that ran the place would turn on one of the projectors. There's no crows on those, though, they warned. They didn't seem to realize that crows weren't the most interesting thing to everybody.

കം കം കം

Soren was at the docks, pants rolled up around his knee, doing a bit of fishing in the hopes of conserving cash. A boat approached and pulled into the docks in rocky fits and starts. A raccoon emerged and waved at him, whistling. Soren stared for a bit. The boat rocked and seemed to drift away again, then came back and the same raccoon waved again and so Soren went to see what the fuss was.

"Do you know ropes?" the raccoon shouted. "Just what I've seen others do," said Soren.

"Good enough. We'll toss you some sardines and clamshells if you'll help us."

Soren had taken up a variety of knot-tying practices to see if he might make his way into the raccoon fishing trade, but it hardly mattered. He took the end of the rope tossed at him and, in an improvised impression of a longshoreman, he secured it to a steel beam rising out of the wooden dock. The ship came still.

Five raccoons came out from the boat. They were visitors from a distant island, they announced, and they wondered if this was a friendly town for raccoons.

"It's actually almost all raccoons," said Soren. "I'm the rare one here. So, what you heard is probably true. You hardly ever see foxes or badgers, though sometimes, I suppose, since the city is close by. Smaller mammals, mostly. But what you've heard is true. This is a raccoon town and operates under raccoon law."

"So, what brings you to fish in a raccoon city?" a raccoon asked. Soren shrugged and told them he had some concerns with the way foxes did things, and he wasn't so sure if he could ever live happily as a fox in the fox city.

The group listened and shared some sardines and sat by a tree near the docks, resting up.

At first, Soren told them, he was very much drawn to outfoxing everyone. Being as foxy as he could be. He studied Fox Law and became very good at it, which got him up to be a barrister before the Fox Council called upon him for public service in the government, helping to ensure that the rules of the

Fox Council were following arcane Fox Law, particularly on the use of fox magic, and keeping compatible with interphylum treaties.

He never really felt a part of things there, though, and whenever he found himself acting true to himself he felt he would only alienate himself from the other foxes. He shared the story about his antlers.

A raccoon named Crispin listened intently.

"I understand exactly what you mean," said Crispin. "My father got the Disease and died when I was very young. My mother and I moved into a fox property, and it was a terrible thing. She shacked up with the fox and ended up learning a bit of fox magic."

"Interesting," said Soren.

"But she was very concerned with me growing up and learning from other foxes. She wanted me to stay a raccoon. So, my childhood was very happy. I grew up with a regular gaze of kits around me."

"Oh my!" exclaimed Soren. "This is such a familiar story."

"You know how it ends I guess?" asked Crispin.

"My father was a lawyer just like me, but usually out of the house. My mother had six children, and she kept us, always, in the house or the garden. But she always had the habit of having dinner with us, one by one, and only I ever had dinner with father. When I was a bit older, the skulk of us would go for a wander without my parents and my mom always knew if there was trouble when we went out..."

Crispin nodded. "I sense this is coming to the same conclusion." The other raccoons were frustrated. "Tell us!" they shouted.

"OK," Soren started again. "Once I turned to go to law school, I realized I had never really had friends outside of my family, and I wanted to have a bit of independence. I regret to say I didn't come in touch with them very often, though they would come by and leave notes and ask me to come around more. But I didn't, for a few years, I have to say. I was immersed in school and politics and new friendships. When I graduated, I came to visit my parents and the skulk. That's when something very strange happened. I asked about them all: Acke, Benkt, Dagfinn, Fannar, and Frode. She asked who I was talking about."

"What!" they all exclaimed.

"I thought she was making a point that I'd been gone for so long. But she wouldn't tell me a thing about them, and acted like they never existed. I looked at family portraits; it was only ever me. It was a very mysterious thing. So, I apologized and told her that I must being going mad because I could have sworn I had five brothers who would always pester me about doing the right thing and keeping me out of trouble. Well, my mother insisted that there was only one child, and it was me. When my dad came in, I didn't mention it. I thought he'd think I was crazy. But the entire time I couldn't think straight at all. Where had my brothers gone? I began to look for evidence around the house, but then realized that the garden wasn't a real garden at all, just a small porch with some grass."

"So," said Crispin, "What happened? How did you sort it out?"

"Well," Soren started, "I filed it away in the back of my head, and then went out and began working. My father had grown ill, and so I had to come around often to move some boxes around, or do some household tasks. One day a little fella, not much older than a cub, came to me with great curiosity and I asked who he was. 'Soren,' he said, though I'd never told him my name, 'It's me, Soren.' I didn't know any Soren. And then the pup began insisting that he was my brother, which didn't make sense, because my own name was Soren. Why would my mother name us both Soren? I didn't fuss about it, and we moved the painting or mirror or whatever. And then my parents came home, and I asked them about Soren.

"Soren," they said. "This is Soren." I didn't understand. I told them that *I* was Soren. "Yes, you're Soren," said my father. "And this is Soren. He's our son."

"I began to look at the pup and realized he was me. He was me, just about halfway the age I was born to when I'd left. And Soren, I was told, had always been there. I didn't remember him, but whenever I would go to the house, I would eat dinner with little Soren, whom my mother doted on. But he never seemed to age."

"When my father's health worsened, I began spending the night, and so I would sleep in Soren's room, which was actually my old childhood bedroom. Everything just like my own: My spelling trophies, my poster for Vulpine Ball. I woke up one night to find that Soren was absent. I went to look for him, as it was quite late, but I couldn't find him anywhere. I went back to the bedroom and saw just a small fox toy, which I reckoned was his. I scrambled to wake my mom and dad. My mom woke, but father didn't. He'd died in his sleep; and we suspected that Soren had discovered it and ran away in fear or sadness."

"This doesn't sound like Crispin's story at all," said another Raccoon.

"I'll get there, sorry for the diversions," Soren apologized. The raccoons settled in.

"A few years went past and whenever I would talk to my mom she would lament the loss of Soren. Where was her baby Soren? Where did her child go? Would her child ever come back?"

"It became hard to talk about anything else, so I focused on my work to please her. As a result, I got quite far ahead in the legal field. But I could never distract my mother from the loss of Soren. I had long given up on trying to sort out the loss of my older brothers, who I missed dearly, but my mother insisted there was no such thing, so I ignored that sadness and focused on my mother's sadness over the loss of Soren, whom I had never even remembered."

"Well, a bit after that, my mother got sick as well, and when she was on her deathbed she looked at me and asked, "Where is Soren? Where is my baby Soren?" I could never find him. She told me that I must find him, and I promised I would. Then she died. But I have never been able to discover how to find him on my own, and so I hired one of those witch vixens with the dog skulls to come and see if she could see where he was, and she told me something that was rather obvious, in hindsight: I'd been hexed with an illusion magic. Growing up I was surrounded by tricks of my mother's making, a group of friends who were actually all her, split up through illusion magic. My father may have never even known, since I was the only one who needed to see them. And it became apparent that after I'd left home, my father had hexed my mother with an illusion magic, creating a second Soren to replace me. My mother really believed in him, and would never know that she hadn't had two children. He disappeared the day my father died because the spirit of his creation had dissolved with him when we died. It's true of tools and buildings, but also true of magic."

"When my parents died, I was disillusioned, and the magic had no hold on me. But I had memories instead, which are a spirit of their own, a spell we cast upon ourselves."

"Indeed," said Crispin, who then went to hug Soren. "That's precisely my story. I had no brothers, just my mother's secondhand fox magics. But I'll tell you something, you have a home with us!"

The other raccoons cheered.

"Provided you can do some work," chimed in Hellion, an injured raccoon. "You see, our boat failures are a result of an injury I made to my leg. We can't get anywhere until I heal up, and I can't heal up here."

Crispin nodded. "You don't think you could find us a place to stay, do you?"

Soren immediately thought of the musicians he'd met on the first day. He said he'd come right back and see if he could find a spot for them.

He found Mr. Buxton, the bass player, and told him of the traveling raccoons. But Mr. Buxton's band was hesitant to trust a fox with an antler claiming to be the raccoon with an antler they'd jammed with earlier in the week. Soren had forgotten if it was his true form that played with them or some disguise. Now he regretted the decision.

"Surely not all foxes are immune to hospitality, Mr. Buxton."

"I'm sorry. Foxes have some good individuals, but they have very bad structures. And even the very good foxes have lost track of the difference between themselves and their laws. You may well be a good fella, and I wish you the best, but this town keeps to itself for a reason, and that's to keep clear of fox magic as best we can."

Soren understood this very well and found it to be quite a reasonable position. He went back to the raccoons at the boat to give them the bad news.

"Wait," said Hellion. "You went to them as a fox? What if you go back as a raccoon?"

"Oh," said Soren, sheepish. "I don't really do that anymore. It's part of what makes me not so fond of being a fox, if I'm being honest."

"Is it against the law?" asked Hellion.

"No, no, but see, that's just the thing," Soren started. "I suppose I'm a strong advocate of Fox Law protections across Phylums, that is, for us foxes to regulate not only our own rules but the agreements of behavior with others..."

"A pan-animal law!?" shouted Hellion, who seemed appalled. "Don't presume you should tell others how to be treated. That's quite presumptuous."

"Well, no one likes to be tricked..."

"But you can't stop everyone from being a fool. The only pan-animal law is not to kill and even that has been negotiated to be a rule of each phylum."

"I don't mean to get political," said Soren. "I digress."

"Surely," said another raccoon, "You don't mean to say that some moderate adjustments to your presentation isn't the same as ganging up on an herbivore to tear it to shreds with your teeth?"

"No, I suppose not," said Soren. "I'm sorry, it just doesn't feel right."

Crispin intervened.

"Everyone, let's respect our friend. He was kind enough to help us with our ship, and we have already asked too much of a stranger." Crispin began making plans to accommodate sleeping in the ship. Hellion could sleep in the more comfortable sleeping quarters and one raccoon per night would take the other bed, the rest rotating through dock sleep.

"No way," said Hellion, "We're all brothers here." Then, looking at Soren: "Well, not all. But. I'll take part in the regular rotation."

Soren saw his pipe dream of joining the band of raccoon brothers slipping away.

"Wait," he said, overcome with guilt. "I'll do what I can. If I tell them I'm one of you guys, it's not a lie, right? I'll go and tell them, as a raccoon, that I'm part of a traveling band of fishermen and that we need a place to stay. If they don't ask if I'm a fox, well, I don't have to lie."

The raccoons cheered.

"That's great, Soren," said Crispin. "You really are one of us."

Soren took raccoon form in the flicker of an eye. He tucked his tail into his fisherman's robe.

"Uhm," said a raccoon. Hellion saw it too.

"What?" asked Soren.

"The antler. If you don't want to raise suspicion that you're secretly the antlered fox that needs a place for a bunch of raccoons to stay, you shouldn't show up as an antlered raccoon with an identical proposal."

Soren was quiet for a thought.

"Why don't YOU just go?" he asked.

"I'm injured!" He pointed to his furry ankle, which had specks of blood. "And you know these people. You can sweet talk a deal."

Soren sighed and removed his antler headband. He looked just like any other raccoon now.

He turned to Crispin and told him how important the antlers were to him.

"I'm trusting you to look after them," Soren said.

"I understand," said Crispin. "It is hard to trust someone after living and growing up in a world where fox magic has made reality seem so malleable, constantly shifting into crazy and unsettled truths. But we raccoons live closer to the dirt. We value a solid place to keep our feet after a journey out to sea. Rest easy, your prize is safe with us!"

And so, Soren returned to Mr. Buxton's as a raccoon. It was getting late in the night and they were already preparing for their nesting. Mr. Buxton was worn down from the evening and said sure, sure, fine, but then invoked raccoon law to invoke a truth.

"Sure," swallowed Soren.

"A fox fellow came by earlier with a similar tail, and I need your assurances, under raccoon article five, that your group is not a band of disguised foxes intent to make havoc."

"No sir," said Soren, relieved at the exact legally binding structure of the question. "This group is not a group of disguised foxes intent to make havoc."

"Very well then," said Mr. Buxton. "I'll pull up some grass for them. They can rest here for the rest of the day and when we wake for the evening we'll discuss a longer stay."

The traveling raccoons were elated and cheered and packed enthusiastically when Soren delivered the news. Soren asked Crispin for his antler, but Crispin noted he'd already packed it and wouldn't it be weird to show up with an antler now? Soren agreed that it was not worth the trouble for Crispin to unpack something he'd have to hide anyway and then went to help Hellion carry his bag.

The sun had started rising and so the traveling raccoons arrived in the hazy blue hues of dawn. On the walk, one had started pounding a drum, and they all shared a batch of Wolf Mead. Soren was a bit tense, as this was not the kind of thing that was conducive to a nice sleep.

They arrived at Mr. Buxton's and settled immediately onto piles of grass bedding that he had set aside for them, offering only curt greetings to the host.

"I suppose you're all very excited to come upon such great hospitality that you've lost sight of yourselves," said Soren. "But perhaps a moment of thanks is due for Mr. Buxton."

A roar of cheers went up and the raccoons held up their pint glasses of Wolf Mead. One of them wrapped his arm around Mr. Buxton and started a long round song of bawdy raccoon praise.

"He's a bit of a shit, this kit, this kit,
But everyone's git' to make peace with it,
Cuz his bit is a hit when you're down in the shit
And no shit kit could be more fit
Than old {name's} waaaaaaaays."

The song inserted Mr. Buxton's name in its traditional place. Mr. Buxton smiled good naturedly but was confused and a bit worried about his sleep.

"All right then everyone, let's tuck in and I'll hear all of your undeserved gratitude in the evening over some eggs," he said.

"Yes, yes," Soren weakly chipped in, "early to bed, early to rise!"

One of the raccoons had found the jug jam jazz band's instrument closet and was passing around an assortment of kazoos and other wind instruments. The cacophony of a student band room before a practice emerged, but it never coagulated into music.

"We're jaaaaaaaazzzzz musicians," said one raccoon quite loudly, and the room burst into laughter as if some mean-spirited seal had just been broken on their drunkenness. They ordered Mr. Buxton to go get them some more mead. Embarrassed, Soren volunteered to run the task.[10]

On his walk he worried that he did not want to be part of the group anymore, now that he had seen their ugly side, but also worried that the group may not want him once they knew he wasn't ugly. He feared, too, that Mr. Buxton would discover his secret. He hurried over to a wooden food cart being dragged home by the slowest raccoon of the evening, and ordered all the mead he could get with the combined income from his stints as a musician and haphazard longshoreman. Now he was broke, but this was the price he paid to keep his secret.

He could hear the wailing of woodwinds and pounding of drums, punctuating a roiling chorus of whooping laughter. He was dismayed to find the house he'd hurried home to was now full of foxes. He dropped two bottles of mead to the ground, which shattered on the floor.

Their reverie was hardly good-natured. He saw one of them wearing Soren's antler, fashioned to emerge from his pants like a branchy penis.

"Soren!" they cheered.

"I'm not Soren," he answered, with poor strategy.

---

[10]*"Ego is a structure that is erected by a neurotic individual who is a member of a neurotic culture against the facts of the matter. And culture, which we put on like an overcoat, is the collectivized consensus about what sort of neurotic behaviors are acceptable." - Terence McKenna*

"No?" said the fox with the antler phallus. "Then... *Where's my baby Soren?*" The foxes burst into laughter. Soren felt humiliated and angry.

"Stop this!" he shouted. "You're not just being rude to me, but also to your host, who has nothing to do with whatever game you're trying to win. You've destroyed Mr. Buxton's home and you've got no reason."

"We have reason," said a fox, who Soren recognized as Peter. "As you know, breaking a promise has penalties. You took an oath to public service and when you disappear on your little raccoon jazz holiday you leave a lot of people in the lurch. We depend on you not to go off undocumented, Soren! And so, when we realized how much extra time we'd been taking to get your work done, we decided to take a little vacation of our own."

"I do appreciate that a promise is a promise," said Soren. "I should have been clear to you about what I was doing. For breaking that promise, I apologize. But you've got no right to take it out on Mr. Buxton."

"Well, Mr. Buxton," Peter turned to him, "Soren here informed us that you were very interested in hosting a fox party. We offered him lots of cash to share with any proprietor willing to share open space for our weekend jazz-and-mead vacation, and he said he'd hand it off to you. I'm not sure, but it seems like the two of you need to work out that payment, as it seems Soren has not been forthcoming, but we will not be moving on until we are reimbursed for our payment plan. You see, we were offered housing by a secondary agent under false pretense."

"You gave me no such fee," said Soren. "And I made no such agreement. You'll not be getting any payment from me tonight, I'm afraid."

Peter shrugged and told the foxes to take the musical instruments to the boat and that they'd be leaving ("Diurnal," he offered in a patronizing explanation to Mr. Buxton). The foxes all tipped their hats to Mr. Buxton on their way out, but their politeness did not hide the wreckage of the place they'd left behind.

"We'll be off with the repayment fee in the form of your musical instruments, then, Mr. Buxton. Soren, will you join us? Or will you abdicate your responsibilities to your Phylum for yet another week?"

Soren said he would not be going.

Soren and Mr. Buxton stood in silence, listening to the distant zip of the raccoon (now fox) boat. Soren began to pick up around the den. Mr. Buxton asked him to stop and please to leave. So, he did.

4. SOPHIE WATCHES A MOVIE

"石," part 1.

Sophie told the pigeons she had no preference among the six theaters. They sent her to theater four and dimmed the lights.

It was a black and white film and the people spoke a different language, but the text would appear at the bottom of the screen as they spoke.

The film opened on a small villager's home, crafted out of wood with sliding paper doors, nestled among towering bamboo and rice paddies. A man who lived inside the home wore a robe but no shoes. His face was tired and dirty. He called from a porch.

"石!" he shouted. He was calling for someone.

Next, Sophie saw a little girl deep within a muddy, empty well. She was sifting through the mud for something. It was an abandoned well, used by passing fishermen to clean their catch. When the traveling fishermen would pass through, they often let hooks fall into the well as they gutted the fish. 石 would descend into the well to retrieve the hooks. Her father would bend them into their original form, and then sell them back to the passing fishermen.

石 heard her father's cry and placed the hooks carefully between her front teeth. The camera was positioned at the bottom of the well, and the stark black and white revealed only a white circle until it was interrupted by her silhouette. She climbed up the well, then over, her bare feet hitting wet soil. She spit the hooks into her hands, and ran to her father, who had prepared for her a bowl of rice and an entire pink fish.

"Today is your seventh birthday," he said, "So today you get the whole fish."

石 smiled, then tore the fish in two with her hands, placing it on top of her father's bowl of rice. He smiled and they ate together in silence.

In the morning a half-eaten chicken carcass appeared on the stairs just as 石 went to fetch eggs.

"A fox," said her father. He told 石 to fetch some wood. He pulled what remained of chicken meat from the bird, and built a trap.

The screen turned to night time, and the air filled with a drone of cicada. Through the window, 石 and her father sat in silence, eating rice without meat. Then the sound of wood collapsing on a stone. The father rises from the table to see.

He slides open a sliver of wood, revealing the eyes of a fox.

"Honorable fox," the man says, "I'm sorry but you have taken away my eggs. I see you left us half a chicken, but we will eat for a day and starve for a year. What can you do to make amends?"

"My kits are starving," the fox said, though Sophie could only see his eyes. "You know a fox is loyal to those who show it kindness. I can protect your daughter from her fate."

石's father stepped back and took out a sword.

"A fox's threat is always a trick," he said.

The fox tossed himself around the box.

"That's bad wisdom," the fox said. Sophie thought about it. It's true, she'd never heard a Fox Law saying such a thing about threats. Humans, perhaps, hadn't worked very hard to understand the rest of the Phylums. Maybe they didn't care much about Fox Law at all!

石's father pushed the sword into a small slit that had been cut into the trap for just this purpose. The sound of the fox's scream and 石's formed a union. The screen faded to darkness.

Then:

the sound of a drum;
the white circle of the well, seen from beneath;
the sound of 石 climbing;
another strike of the drum;
the circle turns black.

We heard only 石's breaths, and a pitiable moan of fear hummed through her lips, closed tightly around the hooks between clenched teeth. She had gone blind at the bottom of the well.

She moved her hands to lift herself from the pit, but without sight of the next highest stone, she knew she would slip. She tried to work from memory. Dirty hands grasp for cracks in stone, and then darkness filled with the soft thud of her body hitting the earth. Silence and darkness lingered in the theater for so long, Sophie wondered if the film had ended.

The rectangle becomes bright with the face of 石's father staring out, still and sad.

Her lips are bleeding around a hook lodged into her tongue. Her father twists the steel around it. Sophie thinks it looked so much like the fish they shared on her birthday. 石 is crying, but her eyes show no expression, just stare straight into the near distance.

The hook slides around, then out. He adds it to a pile of four hooks on a piece of wood stained with blood-painted fingerprints.

石 cannot speak or see. The screen turns white. 石, healthy, walks toward a cherry tree. She speaks, but her mouth doesn't move.

"I began to withdraw into the sweetness of my memories. My childhood became a sanctuary, a world which deepened in beauty and detail as I froze my memories in time to examine them. In truth, the beauty of these cherry blossoms lasted only ten days, when I was six. But in the silence of my quiet study, in the refuge of my inner world, they lasted a hundred days and more. And then my father died."

A holy man passes 石 a bone with chopsticks. He moves her hand to receive it.

From then, 石 was reliant on the kindness of a Shinto priest. He brought her two small oranges and a bowl of rice each morning. 石 returned one orange to him each time, as gratitude.

One day, an old woman came to her from the mountain. She was blind herself. She offered 石 an amulet, and asked if she had spoken to her father.

石 could not respond, but thought to herself that it was a silly question. Her father was dead.

The mountain woman began to scatter salt. Then she played the koto. With each pluck, she chanted the name of a God. Then she stopped. A low humming sound swelled from a source that Sophie couldn't see. The woman began to sing, but the tone of the hum was consistent.

"Now then,
How auspicious,
How wonderful!
When spring comes to this house
The blossom and in the fall
The fruits ripen, still!
In the gardens
We take the pearls
And peacocks!
1,002 birds!
From peacocks,
The mountains,
Four directions wide,
We at once recite
JANJARA."

A loud drone behind this chant rose from the soundtrack. Sophie could not understand it, or the meaning of this song.

石 returned to the cherry blossom. Peacocks filled the sky and the ground. From outside of this world, the woman continued her song, breaking in.

"The stones become pebbles,
And moss grows upon them
With reins of moss
Now, this house
He deigns to bless."

石 saw a stone, covered in moss. It was new in this remembered world. The disembodied voice of the mountain woman asked her, "What do you see?"

"A stone, covered in moss," she said.

"Suck from the moss' marrow."

石 did as she was told. She put her mouth upon the moss and sucked deeply from the stone. She looked upward, and saw her father.

"I am watching over you for now," he said. "But so much harm awaits you. I cannot be your witness forever."

He pointed directly to the screen; to Sophie. So did 石.

"They are with you now," he told her.

Sophie grew uneasy. The screen went black. The mountain woman whispered:

"The old fox in the Shinoda woods, when he cries in the day, he does not cry at night."

"The old fox in the Shinoda woods, when he cries in the day, he does not cry at night."

"The old fox in the Shinoda woods, when he cries in the day, he does not cry at night."

"石," part 2.

I went with the mountain woman to the foothills surrounding Mount Osorezan. Her name was Satsuki.

Every day Satsuki recited prayers and I would repeat them as I ran my fingers over papers, which soon I was taught to fold into amulets. Each 17 days Satsuki went to town for three days and earned her living selling these amulets and speaking to the dead. She came back with food, usually rice.

When she was away I would practice koto, which I learned to play by touch. If I did not play perfectly, I could not eat. I always learned the song perfectly.

Sometimes I returned to the world within myself, but the call of Satsuki had rendered away the memory and complicated it with peacocks and the moss-covered stone. I had to drink from it, every time, as if I was compelled. I never saw my father there again. The blossoms let go of their tenuous grip upon the branches, and I could not imagine them, or remember them, back into existence. Soon, there was no refuge there. I believed that you, the reader of this story, were no longer reading.

One day, Satsuki returned from town with a dog and told me he would keep me company when she was gone. I could not see him but I comforted myself by running my fingers over his thin coat. He was a small dog and I could hear his breath and I would imagine him smile, though I had never seen a dog smile, have you? The idea of him was something to imagine now that I could not remember even the imagination of the cherry tree.

Satsuki always asked if I could think of his name. I never could. She said that it was important that I hear him speak his name. I thought the idea of a talking animal was silly but then I remembered the fox.

There is a difference between imagination and sense, Satsuki told me. It is easy to imagine a name from within me, a name for the feelings the animal calls out. In fact, it was true. I always imagined the name of the dog was the name of my father. But that was just a wish. A wishful thing isn't knowledge.

Satsuki was in the village one day when I put my fingers in his fur and saw the cherry blossom. I could see him and I knew I could see him, because he looked distinct from when I had imagined him. He told me his name.

"His name is Mei," I told Satsuki when she returned. She was pleased.

"The world can speak to us," she said. "But we have forgotten how to ask questions. We have forgotten how to listen to things." She said the only way to hear the world was to break ourselves of the noise of being human. She said that now that I was 12 I was ready for my final year of testing.

The first passage was the *inugami*, she said. She said she was sorry for what would happen.

Sophie watched as Satsuki took a shovel and dug a hole about four feet deep by two feet wide. She lowered Mei into the hole, so only his head was rising above the grass, and then returned the soil. A heavy piece of wood was placed over the repacked soil and weighed down by stones. Mei began to look around, confused, and then began to whine.

Satsuki tied 石 to a wooden pole so she couldn't move, and left for three days.

石 could only hear the whining of Mei, but didn't understand what was wrong. Mei was facing her, and cried for three days. 石 could only offer assurances. And then she tried to hear him.

Satsuki returned with a piece of horse meat she'd obtained as payment for her necromancy, and laid it in front of the dog. Mei could see it, but not reach it. He barked, and salivated, and whined, and began to growl. He had not eaten in three days.

Satsuki fed me *miso*, and explained that Mei's life force would become concentrated in his skull, because he would be so focused on moving only his head to the carrion. His life would focus on his sight of me, and the meat, full of willful desire for both. When he died, she said, all of this life force would be concentrated in the bones of his skull. His skull would lure his spirit back to me for as long as I held it. This would become a talisman for the next stages of my training.

Satsuki left for three more days. The room was only the sound of Mei's whine, my sobbing, and the increasing buzz of flies as they descended upon the horse flesh. Soon Mei was silent, and I heard only the flies beyond my tears. I realized they were landing upon the carcass of Mei.

"石," part 3.

When Mei died I could never return to the cherry tree again. All that remained was the moss-covered stone and a pile of dead and rotting peacocks. The stone grew larger over time, and took up all the space inside of me. For a while, I could look backward, to the cherry tree, but instead of blossoms I would see the hanging, rotten corpse of my father. Sometimes I saw the emaciated body of Mei, dragging his own corpse by tossing the weight of his head forward; his own limbs useless.

That's when Satsuki began the ceremony of *mizugori*. It was winter. I was stripped bare and tied to a wooden beam. Satsuki and another mountain woman took turns taking buckets of freezing water from the stream and tossing the water out onto what felt like my corpse. I was told to repeat the sutras I had memorized, 100 times. When I finished, I was to sing the song about the insects and the birds and hell. One hundred times after that, I would recite the New Year's ritual, and then the *kamioroshi*, a song about a girl and a horse that dies and then comes back to rescue her. One hundred times each. If it was imperfect, I would start again.

I only slept when I fainted, and this became frequent. I was fed a cup of rice in the morning and a cup of matcha in the evening and a sip of vinegar if I looked about-to-die. I was told to chew on a strip of cedar, upon which they had carved a prayer.

When I had recited these songs 100 times while receiving the ablutions, three days had passed. They took me to my bed and wrapped me in a blanket and offered me miso and tea.

I slept for nearly a day. Satsuki woke me at three in the morning and told me that the training was finished and now it was time for the wedding to the spirit.

I was dressed in a white kimono. My body was sore and broken. My skin was wrapped tight around my skeleton. I was taken back to the water, and as I heard the gurgle of the stream I lost all fight. I was overcome with despair and heartbreak. I thought that even one more moment of this was unbearable; but was most terrified that this was infinite. I had no power over the course of my life but to be captive to sadists. They tortured my body and invaded my memories and filled my childhood with death. They had encouraged me to love specifically to torture whatever I would love. They conspired to destroy every precious thing that could blossom within me.

All I could do was scream and cry, but soon even that was gone. To scream and cry draws upon some well of hope that had become exhausted. I remembered myself at the bottom of the well by my father's house, a dry well. A cold burst of water cut across my face. This was despair.

Satsuki shouted. Just as I had learned the name of Mei, she said, I must come to learn the name of the spirit I would marry. This would not come from one source, like Mei's name came to me, but would come from all the sources available to me. The spirit would shout it, unmistakably.

The sting of liquid needles on my back felt as if it passed through me, carrying specks of flesh set loose from the bone. The sound of water upon the ground could just as well have been the sound of my flesh and blood and entrails. I became bored by my pain. This was not stoicism or transcendence. It was complete resignation to my body's disintegration.

What was left of me, I wondered? And then there was nothing left of me.

The film stopped, and a pigeon came out and told Sophie he was sorry, but the theater was closing.

5. TRAGEDY AT THE BORDER

Soren had never been good at reading the forest, or understanding what it was trying to tell him. He entered it with the weight of solitude. He'd stayed in the Raccoon Grotto for a bit, trying to find work. Only a few days of averted glances and quiet, businesslike greetings convinced him that he had become a living confirmation of fox arrogance.

Though Soren was a creature of the forest, it didn't provide him any sense of homecoming. His life was among streets and the buzzing clamor of shopkeepers, and the forest offered nothing more compelling than his own failure.

Soren felt his boundaries then, and as he ruminated on the humiliations he'd endured, he felt the edges of his fur sharpen. He felt distinct and separate in his sadness, but solid, too. Misery was a weight he could tie his tail to, lest he otherwise float away.

He wrote a letter.

Dear Soren,

Why would the world go ahead and make a creature that thought it was always alone? But that's what happened. We're born and at first the fur on our arms is just part of some incomprehensible goopy world. A paw here, the end of a snout. Your mom's eyes. Your father's ears. A den to burrow in, a tree, a stone. None of it distinct at all. The end of your snout may as well be the branch of a tree.

Then something happens. You say, "Here I am!" and there you are. But what have you done, really? You've just found the spot where your fur ends and the air begins, and you name it, and then for the rest of your life you're some separate, solitary chunk of fur. And the stone has its own name.

Except you, Soren. Do you have your own name or just mine? What a meaningless meaningful question. What are you, really? Just the name, answering to the call of other people's questions? You didn't even choose your name. But none of us do.

They call your name as if you can answer, but they are the ones who named you. And they ask you questions as if you can answer, but they're the ones who told you the answers!

For the duration of the life I've lived under this name, and always worked to answer it better. To answer the law that my father wrote, that the foxes taught me. But I never had my own name. I never had my own language. I never created my own laws.

They tell you that if you listen to the law, if you follow the words they tell you, that you will find yourself where they are. And just as they named you and you answered to the name and they gave you the answers to the questions they asked, they also told you the thing you wanted and then you wanted it when you were asked what you wanted.

Oh, some of us stay so much closer to the forest than others! Some of us don't even know how to live here anymore. Because we have a name that they've given us, and a set of answers about who we are that helps us keep the edges of our fur distinct from the air that surrounds it.

My father stole my name and gave it to you. I don't know who you are, but I am supposed to find you. But I am looking for Wolf Mead, and a set of antlers. Then I will find my name.

Sincerely yours,
Soren 1

Just as Soren crossed out the 1, he heard the commotion of wolves in the distance.

ح   ح   ح

Outside of the cinema, Sophie looked back to the tree. She did not approach it. She didn't think very hard about why, but she knew that staying here was an indulgence. She bowed to the tree, and then she returned to the raccoons she rode in with.

The boat was stopped by a raccoon in a blue robe as the crew was tying rope to the pier. The raccoon said he needed to inspect their tails. The raccoons, confused, complied nonetheless.

The guard turned to Sophie with special attention, and asked the purpose of her visit.

"I'm meeting my friend. A fox named Soren."

"Tail, please!" the guard shouted, his attention refocused.

Sophie turned her tail for inspection. It was more demeaning for her than the other raccoons.

"Soren Fox and his associates are not welcome in Raccoon Grotto," the guard said. "What is your association with him?"

"Just a friend," Sophie said.

"He's a criminal involved in the theft by deception of 16 musical instruments," the raccoon managed to sound like he was shouting without raising his voice. "They stole brass whirly tubes and a handful of rub-tubs from Mr. Buxton," he barked. "The whole town is silent now."

"I don't know anything about it, but that doesn't sound much like Soren."

The other raccoons began to apologize to the guard. Then they doubled down by scowling at her and saying that she should have said she was messed up with criminals. They'd never have brought her here.

"You are denied entry to the Raccoon Grotto until restitution is paid to Mr. Buxton on behalf of Mr. Soren Fox, Esquire," the guard said.

Sophie looked around.

"Do I swim?"

The guard agreed to escort her to the border of the town, though the borders were quite loose. He'd take her to the road, which seemed as good a border as any.

Sophie had never been to Raccoon Grotto, so she did not know that the streets were usually full of music and good cheer. The Raccoons she passed would be smiling to one another but then restrain themselves as she passed, as if they didn't want to be caught in the vulnerability of their own happiness.

At the road, Sophie asked which way Soren was expected to have gone. They pointed up the road, away from the bridge. As they turned their attention to the road, they saw, in the distance, a pack of dogs and wolves running toward them. A steady flow of dogs arrived; a giant pack of about 30, then a pack of 10, then a pack of 5 smaller dogs struggling to keep up.

The raccoon guards shouted at them to stop at the road which had now become established as a border. The Wolf Union seemed to stop there anyway.

A wolf emerged to speak. His words were repeated by the dogs behind him, and then repeated by the dogs behind them. That way everyone could hear. The effect was a booming echo of sound.

"You have been prohibiting dogs from entering your Grotto, which violates the right to free travel." "You have been prohibiting dogs from entering your Grotto, which violates the right to free travel." "You have been prohibiting dogs from entering your Grotto, which violates the right to free travel."

"That's not true," the raccoon guard repeated. He was startled to find his answer echoed, too. He realized that he was in no position to speak on behalf of the raccoons. He asked the other guard to go get the Eldest Raccoon.

"We're on the lookout because Mr. Buxton has been robbed," the raccoon continued.

"We're also told that you've been hiding a number of disguised foxes in your town. I need your assurances under your own article 5 that you are not a disguised fox."

The raccoon thought this sounded oddly bureaucratic for wolves.

"No, I'm not. We're looking for foxes ourselves. A band came by and stole our brass whirly tubes and a handful of rub-tubs from Mr. Buxton," he explained. "We're simply stopping free entry until we see some tails."

This was repeated. The wolf responded:

"We were told that a band of raccoons were forced out of this town, which had been overcome by fox pretenders. They salvaged the instruments to save their own neighborhood."

"That's the opposite of the facts," the raccoon explained. Wolves began to howl. The raccoon guard was relieved to see the Eldest Raccoon was approaching, in his purple robe and blue wizard-cap.

"I am the Eldest Raccoon," he shouted. "And I am afraid you've all fallen for a fox trick. There are no secret foxes here. We've checked every tail of every creature and all are gray with brown stripes or reflecting of whatever tail that animal has by nature. There are no red tails here."

This was repeated.

"Now, you are all welcome to come to our Grotto, but we need to check your tails to be sure you are not violating Article 5 yourselves. If you have nothing to hide you have nothing to fear."

A wolf cried out, "Let's see your tail then."

"I have no need to show you MY tail," the Eldest Raccoon responded. "This a Raccoon Grotto."

A small Lhasa Apso broke from the crowd and tore off the robe of Eldest Raccoon. The dogs went into a frenzy. The tail of the Eldest Raccoon was red.

Sophie understood immediately. But the Wolf Union went into a frenzy as a group of smaller dogs ran to tackle the Eldest Raccoon. They seized his haunches and dangling limbs. They bit through his flesh to force him to reveal his full fox form.

Sophie broke into a run and stormed them. She swiped her antlers wide, and shook some of the smaller dogs, but had to avoid hurting the Eldest Raccoon. But their whimpers became a frenzied howl and all dogs descended to aid their allies.

The Eldest Raccoon was swallowed into a torrent of gnash and incisor. And then, silence echoed outward from a Boston Terrier who, in his mouth, held the gray and black striped tail of a raccoon, torn from Eldest's backside. The dogs immediately went low to the ground, whimpering.

"It's a trick!" Sophie shouted. "A fox illusion of a fox tail, so we would fight!" By then the crowd had sorted it out.

It was all temporary. In the distance, a plume of smoke was rising from the forest, and the dogs were immediately distracted.

6. A BIRD'S GUIDE TO WOLF MEAD

Birds are always compelled by memory. Across all Phylums, they're the ones who live most perpetually in nostalgia. The past isn't just lost time. It's a mechanism in the brain that drives them into movement at the turn of every winter.

A young bird cracks his way through the pearl-colored contours of a tree-high egg, and quickly learns to flit about the sky. Her first pilgrimage is south, to warmth and food. The experience is dangerous. Motion always has risks. Some hawks celebrate their birthday with a feast of migrating birds; mother hawks lay an egg in time to ensure baby emerges to the feast. Imagine passing through the territory of a creature that was born, through design rather than astrological coincidence, to devour you.

She could stay home, this bird, but doesn't. Hunger drives all motion: hunger and nostalgia define the life of birds. You can stay home, motionless, but soon, your body will push you to move. If you resist long enough, stay still long enough to turn enough nows into befores, you'll become overwhelmed with hunger. Desire always rises.

She wakes up and knows it's time to leave. The rest of the birds get ready, too. They know the path, even though they've never flown. They've spent months knowing they would know the time to leave, trusting that, when the time comes, they'll know how to get where to go.

So, they fly.

৶ ৶ ৶

Wolf Mead is a misnomer. It isn't brewed by or derived from wolves. The name comes from its location, central to the territory controlled by the local Wolf Union, a sacred site with a unique ecosystem.

The migrating birds fly past because it's a red-berry paradise. But the berries ripen at a moment when migrants are passing through the territory of emergent hawks. The undevoured survivors descend on the mountain when the berries are slightly overripe. Having passed through the hawk territory, it becomes a rite of passage: Drunk on fermented berries, the birds fly crooked and loop-de-loop around the mountaintop.

Our young bird hero makes her way to Wolf Mountain only by moving through enemy territory. It goes like this: You fly and fly and your friend goes down and that's the only way you know that you didn't. The only warning you have that you're in danger is watching a faster bird grasp its talons around the body of your brother and then tearing open his belly with a beak. That's your warning.

You have to fly faster, already exhausted, and then evade, scoot, dip, all the evasive maneuvers of birds in mid-flight. The survival strategy is not to be strong, or to fight, or to outwit. It's simply to have enough of your brothers and sisters hatch from eggs that they can't eat all of you. Stripped of all poetry, this is the nature of the bird.

You do it every year, and your radar gets off. A tree triggers your trauma, and you wonder if it's a memory or a fear. You're already immersed in remembrance; you only take this journey because of some incomprehensible beacon drawing you to the past, the nest, the womb outside the bird, the womb dangling on the end of a branch as you gestate and then open your maw for worms. Birds are never protected. They are born exposed and vulnerable; their shelters made of shell and spit and the only twigs they could carry. And yet this weakness gives them the power of outrageous courage: the first act of their lives is throwing themselves out of a tree.

When there's a particularly large slaughter, the birds don't get to Wolf Mountain in the same numbers. The berries go uneaten, and ripen to the point of falling off the bush.[11] They roll down the side of the rock into the crevice, and fall into a pile below, where they slowly decompose into the trickling stream.

---

[11] *"The riper they got, the clearer they grew, till you could see the tiny veins in their skins and the seeds and the juice. Each currant hung there like an almost-told secret. Oh! you thought, if the currants were just a wee bit clearer, then perhaps you could see them living, inside." - Emily Carr, The Book of Small. Toronto: Irwin, 1942. P. 56*

Wolf Mead in slaughter years is more potent, and the wolves understand it is simultaneously the result of a tragically interrupted journey home and a celebration of those who made it.

The other thing about Wolf Mead is that there are psilocybin mushrooms in the cave, which grow and degrade into the stream, releasing hallucinatory chemicals into the brew.

The berries mold over and interact with a moss growing in the spring beneath the mountain. This mold interacts with a hallucinogenic mushroom that rises from moss growing under the stones. Falling berries give the water below its tart taste. But the buzzy effects come from the mold growing up from deep beneath the surface. Eating that mushroom on its own was nearly deadly. The rotting fruit makes the psychedelic effects just barely palatable.

Our baby bird lands on the side of a mountain. There's no one else there this season, save for one fox, alone in a basin where our two worlds meet. He is taking water into glass jars. Berries, one by one, plop down into the stream.

Soren had arrived there through a mixture of history, subterfuge, and accident.

When the Wolf Union found him, he was aimlessly gathering sticks for a shelter. It was an odd thing to do, but dogs didn't understand foxes. Threatened by a fox in their territory, the wolves confronted him and he told them his tale.

One of the dogs remembered Soren's bag of leaves from the bridge and said so to the others when he'd come back here. The dogs were impressed with the honest fox, and thanked him for the tip-off. They'd stopped selling to the badger in question, they said, and demanded restitution.

"We were surprised he agreed," they said.

Soren understood that the wolves had probably just been tricked again, given a bag of stones and told it was gold or something. This was just further proof to him of the gullibility of wolves, the kind of dumb trust that lead them to being forced out into the forest instead of the city. Something in him hated wolves for their susceptibility to fox magic, and when his better side tried to explain that fox magic was universally powerful — that he, too, fell for it, and that he, too, was a fox who should know best — his annoyance only deepened.

The wolves told him that they had previously invited honest foxes into their pack. They knew that city foxes tended to be solitary creatures, but if there was some part of him that yearned for a pack, he was welcome. He was already family, they said — though they knew foxes tended not to consider themselves as such.

Soren heard them but was focused, instead, on something that the wolves had let slip by speaking too casually: The wolves he'd met on the bridge had *come back here*. That implied that this was not some roaming hunting party, but may well be the center of the Wolf Territory. Wolf Mountain was nearby.

Soren nodded and pretended to listen as the wolves spelled out the benefits of life in the union. Brotherhood, they said, was a powerful connection.

No wolf is ever alone, unless they want to be. They work together and play together.

The more they spoke, the more Soren calculated. He briefly wondered what he was doing. But he answered it quickly: He was a fox. His only skill was swindle and his only tool was tricks. The greatest act of kindness would be to convince them further not to trust a fox.

"You know," Soren interrupted. "I met five raccoons in the Grotto, and all five were foxes in disguise."

It was a non-sequitur, but Soren understood that dogs were easily distracted and gullible to illusions. He didn't even have to try to make this a compelling ruse. Wolves are savages and idiots, he thought. They'll fall for anything.

As expected, the pack's ears perked up. They were all too eager to chase down an imaginary stick once Soren had made the gesture of tossing it.

They argued amongst themselves. The Grotto existed as a kind of buffer between foxes and wolves. If they were taking over the Raccoon Grotto, then they were encroaching on the safety of that buffer. And if they were in disguise, they must be planning something.

Perhaps they should send an investigation party? Or perhaps they should all go, in case a confrontation was unavoidable?

Soren figured the dogs would check the tails of the raccoons and all would blow over and, of course, he had operated within Fox Law, because what he had told them was technically true.

Soren was invited to join them. He declined. Once the pack went running, it was as simple as finding the closest cavern. He only needed to listen for the sound of water rising from deep beneath and to the surface.

There it was: a hole in the side of a mossy green stone, colored rusty gold at the mouth. As he entered, the musty scent of the cavern closed his throat, despite the coolness of the spray. He descended to the belly of this rusty orange stone, folding up the legs of his pants and stepping into the water, filling his jars from the red trickle of the stream.

He began to feel woozy, and sat down in the water. His fur stretched out, pulled longer and longer into the stream by flowing water. It reached out, waving like strands of red kelp, and then the fur tips would disintegrate, flowing out of the cave and then entering from the top of the cave as falling red ants flowed into his body, stinging him, but a tingle-bite, reattaching themselves to him as extensions of his fur, until he was simply a conduit for the passage of red berries and ants that pressed into his skin and extended his fur into a lengthening interconnected flow of anty hair-water, red and moist, the goopy cells of his flesh suddenly reconnected to the tiny atomic time-structures of particles in the substrata, particles illuminated and motivated by the world he had forgotten he could ask about not just a world but the one world a circle of spheres surrounding spheres surrounding a glowing spiral of sunlight organism stretching its own red fur so far into his planet and channeling itself through cracks in the cave into plants and ants that devour the leaves and fall into the stream and touch his body and grow the flaming furlight of his body and tail into the water that flows out and expands into the roots of plants and ants and rising toward sunlight as one swirl of fire and fur and water and ant, nurturing the universal now-light of everything in motion and stillness, "Even pausing is an act of motion!" he shouted and held himself completely still to experience it before coming to the realization that he wasn't thinking about his thinking but now he was thinking about his thinking but is that thinking about thinking still thinking about thinking when you think about thinking about thinking he thought and then he heard his name and ran to the opening at the entrance to the cavern and there were Acke, Benkt, Dagfinn, Fannar, and Frode.

✌ ✌ ✌

"We missed you, Soren." Benkt was always the storyteller. "We missed you every fucking day."

Soren knew better. But he didn't much care.

"I missed you, too," he said. The brothers hugged, and Soren wept. "I never thought I'd see you again," he said. "Where did you all go?"

"I met a girl," said Acke. "I moved South, to Rat City. I always meant to write but, you know, I never found the time. I'm sorry."

"I got a job," said Benkt. "I had a great career for a long time, running a boat! I suppose I was so excited by my life at sea that I forgot about our life on land. I'm so sorry, Soren."

"I was so heartbroken by our mother's death," said Dagfinn. "I could never face the idea of seeing you, or dad, or the rest of our family ever again. I got scared. I'm so, so sorry for leaving you alone for all this time."

"I got sick," said Fannar. "I stayed in touch for a few years, you remember. But then I got sick, and I was ashamed to need so much help, and so I went away so my sickness wouldn't burden you. Our mother... I knew you had done so much for her. I couldn't bear to make you do it again."

"I was a drunkard," said Frode. "I was in town the whole time, and I only called you when I was in trouble. Finally, you decided that I should learn better by losing your support. You were right. I recovered. But I was so afraid to relapse that I thought it better never to tell you. I was so afraid that I'd fail again, and to have you see me fail again, I just..."

Soren's tears flowed silently, and he moaned out loud, a primitive fox cry that had long been forgotten by foxes when they abandoned the family of canids to build a civilization. He began pounding his head on a stone, weeping, exhausted.

Acke, Benkt, Dagfinn, Fannar, and Frode comforted him. Together, they built a fire.

"You had all left so suddenly," he said. "Mom and Dad insisted you were never there at all."

"You saw us every day for years!" said Dagfinn.

"I did. And of course, the stories were always real. But I had wanted our childhood to go on forever. Even if you had all remained, where would you be? You'd grow up. But going so suddenly... I searched for you. Like you were ghosts! I looked for your ghosts everywhere. I just wished so much. So much to make it come back. I wanted to wake up and be told that I was tricked! I was desperate. I wanted so badly to be tricked, so that I could come back. To this."

"We love you, Soren. We do remember. We were there, with you."

"I love you, too," Soren whispered. He took a stick from the fire and approached each of his brothers.

He approached Acke, clapped twice, and bowed. He set fire to his feet. They all stood, watching in silence. When Acke was on fire, Soren bowed again, and clapped twice.

He approached Benkt and did the same. Then Dagfinn, then Fannar, then Frode. Finally, he stopped and bowed again, then collapsed.

❧ ❧ ❧

Sophie came to the source of the plumes, but Soren wasn't there. She spotted the open mouth of a nearby cave. Wolf Mead.

Neither was Soren at the source of the stream. But Sophie felt her legs tremble. The ground shivered. All the tiny particles of dust flew upward, to the roof of the cave.

Slate rock came undone around her hooves, drifting off. The stream moss stood tall and straight, then started upward, too, like green and gentle arrows. The water poured skyward, splashing against the roof of the cave, which itself broke free of gravity and began drifting upward to find new orbits. Gravity was failing everything.

The earth beneath her feet streamed into space like so much spilled kitty litter. She nuzzled her nose into her chest to prevent suffocating in a standing burial.

As the sounds settled, she opened her eyes to an empty, infinite space.[12] When she tried to walk she couldn't. She'd step into nothing, push her hoof against nothing, move from nowhere to another nowhere. There was no gravity, and so there was no resistance, and so there was no movement: only feet, looking for footing.

A giant antlered stone sat suspended in the distance. Sophie recognized her. Was this a mirage? A trick? Was the Deerstone's weight so heavy that it outweighed even the *concept* of gravity?

"I sent you letters," Sophie finally whimpered.

The stone was silent, as always.

"I sent you letters!" Sophie shouted. The stone floated a little closer.

"You never read them," Sophie said, out loud, to herself. "You got them, but you never read them."

The stone kept floating around. Sophie took a good look. When Sophie inhaled, the stone got slightly smaller. When Sophie exhaled, the stone expanded, but not so much. It was like sucking the air out of a balloon from a distance. The transformations set loose some dust and stones, which rolled off the Deerstone's contours before drifting gently skyward.

---

12 *Claudine Herrmann explains that "the term 'space' can express very different things: for each of us there exist a physical space and a mental space. These two have in common the fact that they can be invaded." (113). Herrmann, Claudine. The Tongue Snatchers. Trans. Nancy Kline. Lincoln: U Nebraska P, 1989.*

Sophie saw that she could control the siphoning away of its weight, and so she did, in slow, calm breaths. The stone grew smaller and smaller, into a single particle of dust. As it silently floated into the dark horizon, Sophie wept, alone.

In the distance, a rectangular flicker of light emerged. Within it, a human girl stared, pointing at Sophie, her hair over her eyes, her lips not moving, her words filling space.

"石," part 4.

"I could not 'feel myself disappear.' I think this is a half-measure, if there is still something that can feel a disappearance. True disappearance is a complete inversion. Love is present, even in sorrow and in anger. If it disappears completely it becomes something new and terrifying: the *absence of love*."

A black and white cherry tree, a dead dog, the body of 1,000 rotting peacocks, nothing blossoming but the hanging corpse of her father.

"I could not return to the cherry tree. There was no return, because my past was lost. There was no future, because there was nothing left to dream of."

All sound stopped, and the screen became bright yellow. Sophie squinted her eyes, and the yellow slowly dissolved into white. Sophie saw, in full color, a cherry tree full of white blossoms with a hint of pink waiting to emerge. A smiling dog and then a smiling father. 石 appeared in the frame and they all turned to look at Sophie.

"You were my witness," 石 said.

In black and white, the mountain women pour buckets, alternating to create a constant torrent. The cherry tree shivers, and the blossoms all let go at once. From the sky, a stone descends, and for a spark of a second, a blue figure holding a flaming sword.

"*Nittensama!*" shouts 石. The water stops immediately. There is only the gurgling of a stream now. 石 heaves. She is returned to the blanket and sleeps for days.

"*Nittensama*: The name of my husband spirit. The one who descends to dissolve all illusions. He carries a noose in one hand, to drag the unwilling through the pain of disillusionment. He carries a flaming sword to strike down ignorance of reality."

She awakens dressed in red. Red rice and red fish and deep red plums are laid out before her. She cannot see them. She cannot imagine them. She knows they are there, because they tell her so.

A fade to black. Then the lights came up, as if in a theater. Sophie is back at the base of Wolf Rock. She exits into daylight and finds Soren in the center of a circle of burning scarecrows.

      ॐ   ॐ   ॐ

Soren heard the crackle first, then saw the light illuminating the blood vessels in his eyelids. Then, in the distance, he heard his name.

Wolves ran in a frenzy. He ignored them, making his way through plumes of dark choking ash and fire the color of his fur. If Soren had always been acutely aware of where his body ended, the lineup of fox hair and flame blended together to make him one more blaze in the chaos, the center of a galaxy, like the sun, orbiting nothing.

Not so far off was a young pup. Blinded by the flames, Soren could not see him from a straightforward glance. Instead, he had to shield his eyes, relying on his peripheral vision to make truth out of a hazy outline that was engulfed in overwhelming light.

"Soren!" said Soren.

"Soren!" said Soren.

"I'll save you," Soren said.

The young pup climbed to the elder fox's shoulders. They made their way to the top of Wolf Mountain, where the berries had already been burned. They surveyed the landscape. They were in the center, surrounded by the black residue of smoldering ashes. A ring of red flame was chewing its way outward.

Without the trees and leaves and grass the Sorens could see everything the forest had to hide. In one direction, the bodies of his brothers. In another direction, the pans his mother baked pies in. The skulk-tennis poster of his childhood bedroom attached to a soot-covered stone. All the paperwork from his office scattered among the ashes. The Raccoon Grotto's clamshell shakers. Sophie's body; a pile of antlers; the burned-out shell of the Badger Bar. The bodies of foxes; the bodies of wolves; the bodies of raccoons; the bodies of every person Soren had ever met or known or seen or dreamed of. All of them were covered in the ash that covered every other thing in the devastated forest.

Soren began to weep.

"It's OK," said Soren. "This is all there ever was. Each of us is just defined by the gestures we make against it."

"We all want to find a place where time can stop and tell us we belong there. Nobody ever does."

"Soren!"

Soren turned and saw, for just a moment, the burned corpse of Sophie standing in the distance, calling his name. Then the world turned into a flash of light, and then he saw the vision of the fox-with-nine-tails.

Soren opened his eyes again, and saw a light gray ghost snaking between the still-green redwoods and rising to the sky. Dogs ran to and fro, putting out lingering fires.

"I worried you'd never wake up," said Sophie.

Soren sat up and looked around. Off in the distance was a circle of smoldering scarecrows, made from the sticks he had assembled for his den. The surrounding forest was intact, the grass and soil were moist.

"You found your antlers," said Sophie.

Soren felt the top of his head. Two tree branches were strapped to his ears. It was as if they had climbed upon his shoulders and held on.

"Sophie," he said.

"?"

"An honest fox isn't just some kind of fox. It's its own thing altogether."

A Fire in the Forest.

7. A BRIEF HISTORY OF FOX LAW

Fox law predates the departure of the humans and cats. That law had operated in isolation from the laws of other animals. Upon the departure, things fell into chaos. Animals existed, before then, in a kind of amorphous awareness. Each creature possessed a spirit of itself, but their awareness had been limited.

The shock of the human disappearance simultaneously elevated the animals to the space of consciousness once occupied by humans. Animals quickly found themselves divided into two camps: The first sought to emulate human structures. They occupied the major cities, drawing on pre-existing architecture, and inherited the knowledge that humans and cats left behind.

Others left. Notably, those who left the city most quickly were those who had been most dependent on the humans. No species were as close to humans as dogs and cats, but when the humans ascended, the cats went with them. Betrayed and confused, dogs rejected the city completely. Wolf Union was formed to assimilate the wild breeds of human-tinkered genetics that went into dogs worldwide. The wolves had occupied a space between, and so they were accepting of the dogs, who knew of certain rules. They were loyal to one another.

The foxes, though, had already started integrating into cities before the departure. They had worked into a separate kind of observation from cats and dogs: among, but outside.

A set of truces was established early on. Foxes would keep to the city, and wolves would stay to the forest. Individual members could go between these spaces, but they had to respect the rules of both groups when they did. This was the first law.

The rules were then self-established within the animal groups (Phylums, though they threw this word around casually). The Phylums created laws through various means. Laws were created to mute the instincts of predators and protect the interests of prey. Not all of this was related to eating. As is often the case in politics, less powerful unions often negotiated for things that inspired the survival of their species more so than the survival of individual members. Fish, for example, set rules about how many individual kills a school could endure.

Individual wolves were quite bad at following the rules. Foxes cornered a market on arbitrating the balance of laws. Fox Law soon became immense and bureaucratic, and foxes became the first and only species to reinvent the lawyer. All animal trials were initially negotiated in Fox Court, which gave the creatures an advantage in inter-species dealings that was quickly exploited.

Foxes had always had a tendency toward magic that other animals, apart from badgers, rarely understood. Over some generations, the balance of power began to shift to foxes over wolves. Likewise, the legal system became more entrenched into fox control. A de facto Fox supremacy emerged, which lead to a somewhat exploitative relationship between foxes and all other species.

The Fox Council heard testimony presented from a Field Fox and an Honest Fox. The two were titles that reflected their position: A Field Fox negotiated the side of the aggressor, and the Honest Fox negotiated the side of those who charged an offense. Field Foxes and the Fox Council in general saw it in their interest that Honest Foxes were overworked and generally hired for absent-mindedness.

Fox Law grew and grew, and mastering it became an obsession for Honest Foxes. It was the way that foxes were meant to behave, but the rules were so complex. Fox Council members were quick to point to good laws and then interrogate whether the law had been broken based on the application of other rules.

Magic played a role. Fox Law said nothing about magic, but other animals quickly passed some laws to protect themselves against Fox Tricks. This was constantly being brought to Fox Council for amendment, but the process never seemed to end in a clear answer. Sometimes everyone saw one outcome and then discovered that the outcome applied only to very narrow circumstances, or that the decision had never been meant to be interpreted the way it was clearly interpreted when the decision was reached. In any case, the Fox Council set the rules and oversaw their enforcement.

Soren had been tasked with representing all cases brought to Fox Council by non-Fox Phylums. One of the first arguments he made was that perhaps they should not consider all other Phylums as "Non-Fox." This was rejected.

"They aren't foxes, Soren. So what else would we call them?"

"Perhaps all law could be called Phylum Law, and Fox Law could be one category within it. That would make sure that all laws were equal..."

"Sure," said another council member. "But it isn't very foxy, is it?"

"Well it shouldn't be. If we're creating a set of rules for everyone..."

That got the court up in arms.

"We don't create laws for everyone. We create a law for foxes, and we follow rules that make a foxy kind of sense. Any member of a phylum who brings a case against another phylum is simply choosing to do so under our jurisdiction. Likewise, if anyone is bringing a case against a fox to court, they also do so under our jurisdiction."

"But there's a difference there. One gets to choose to use us and for the other it is the only option."

"They should be lucky to be able to bring a fox case to the only court that other Phylums bring their own squabbles to. And then in-fox squabbles are handled by Fox Law. The rest are not Fox Law. It seems very clear. Don't make it more difficult than it is."

"Common sense," the Fox Council said, practically in unison, and struck a gavel. Soren demurred.

Soren had developed a sense of conviction that Fox Law was the one thing separating animals from the old ways, but this came alongside a sense of not being a very good lawyer. His father, also a Fox lawyer, had operated with a previous council and had won some and lost some.

He was, in effect, a mediocre Honest Fox. Soren had hoped to find himself indispensable to the defense of the other Phylums, but was win few lose most. As much as he had studied, the rules of law were immense, and more rules were being generated every month, published in books and placed on a giant stack that had now overcome the essential furniture in Soren's home.

He would find an argument to articulate a position and bring it forward to the Fox Council, which would say that he'd misunderstood the whole thing, and to reference some other section of case law that he hadn't yet received.

His goal of ascending to Fox Council was all-consuming, and he studied the case law to such an extent that he began to have an almost fluent sense of what he needed to do to win a case.

Something had been stolen from a groundhog. The groundhog came to Soren and told him that she believed it had been stolen by Dagrun Lupine, a local fox. Soren had inquired into the nature of the stolen item, to no avail. Nonetheless, he had to take the case to court.

The defending fox had an easy defense: without knowing what had been stolen, they couldn't charge him with the crime. This was common sense, the Fox Council agreed.

But the groundhog would not say what had been stolen, arguing that she knew well that foxes had a way of making false versions of stolen items appear in court and then everyone says oh, it wasn't stolen at all, it was right under your nose, and then you go home and it's a rock vaguely shaped like a rolling pin or whatever and you're left with nothing because Fox Court cases are final and binding. So, no. She would not identify the item.

Soren went to the groundhog's burrow, taking the form of a groundhog, and invited himself into the burrow for a cup of tea. He glanced around the burrow, trying to make some sense of what might be missing. He plied the groundhog with questions about useful household objects; Soren told her he was a trader and would be happy to find something on his next business trip as gratitude for taking him in. She said that she was a dumpling enthusiast and would love any example of a local specialty dumpling he encountered.

Soren-as-groundhog's eye wandered to a small piece of blank paper with a green trim resting upon a cabinet. Mrs. Groundhog saw his wandering eye and quickly stood up, taking the paper and tucking it away.

"What was that?" Soren asked.

"Nothing, and I'll have you mind not to read things you find exposed in people's homes when they offer you the kindness of tea and hospitality," the groundhog replied. Soren apologized. He said he would sleep elsewhere but that he'd nonetheless bring her a thank you present if she didn't mind. The groundhog was tense and sent him on his way.

Soren had to wait a believable amount of time to return with a small bag of crusty dumplings from Rat City that he'd been given by a traveling mouse in exchange for legal advice. He returned to the groundhog's home, again in the form of a groundhog, and gave her the crusty dumpling as thanks. She let him in to share a dumpling. As her back was turned to fix some tea, he quickly he made his way back to the writing desk and found the blank piece of paper, identifiable by the green border around the edge. He stole it, undetected, and left after a cursory sip of tea.

Three days passed with Soren puzzling at the piece of paper. He held it up to the light to see if something had been dimly inscribed; he traced it with his paws to see if there were inklings of writing. On the third day the groundhog came to him with a small child. The child, she said, was the stolen item; but her son had returned!

Soren said that he presumes this means she would like to drop the charges? She said yes, clearly, she was mistaken all along. Her son had just gone on an adventure and she was quite cross, but also delighted to have him back. He had a bad habit of chasing after rabbits and getting lost in all the big trees. It wasn't the first time he'd done it. She owed

Dagrun Lupine an apology, and she would negotiate that through Soren if he didn't mind.

Soren said he'd file the apology paperwork and drop the case, then wished her on her way. Instead, he promptly went to the accused fox's house. Dagrun was not home.

Soren waited, hidden from sight, outside of Dagrun Lupine's home. Sure enough, he caught the fox coming back late. Soren made his way back to the groundhog's burrow.

He did not have to wait long to see the groundhog emerge from the hole and then re-submerge, in a bit of terror. "Miss," said Soren (he had maintained his fox form) "is something the matter?"

Her son was gone again, she said. Soren expressed some panic, too, but this was exactly as he suspected. He fetched the eldest member of the Fox Council as witness and returned to Dagrun's home, pounding on the door.

Dagrun wearily opened it. He was exhausted.

"Why are you harassing me?" he shouted.

"What do you have to say about this?" Soren asked, holding up the blank piece of paper with green edges. Dagrun panicked.

"I've never seen it before," he said. "You can't prove I wrote that."

"Wrote what?" Soren asked. He showed the blank piece of paper to the Fox Council member.

"You see," explained Soren, "only the enchanter would defend against the words written on a blank page."

The Fox Council member was impressed. He started drafting up the paperwork for arrest right away. But Soren was confused. The groundhog soon approached, and Soren explained the situation.

"But then, where is my son?" she asked.

Soren turned to Dagrun, and said he could offer some amnesty if Dagrun would explain what had happened to her son.

"He died," he said. "Years ago."

"Nonsense!" the groundhog cried. "He went out to play just a month ago and never returned until now."

"I'm afraid you're mistaken," said Dagrun. "I ate him. I ate him and then I pretended to be him, so I could enjoy the dumplings you made for him."

"Holy shit," Soren said. "This is a capital..."

"Yes," said Dagrun. "But I'll get away with it."

The groundhog stood ground and said that this was all lies and that she would like to keep the charges dropped. Soren was shocked.

"My son will come home," she said. "You'll see."

Soren had no choice but to drop the case. And sure enough, her son came home. Soren stopped by to see them. The groundhog and her happy child were eating dumplings. Of course, it was always Dagrun Lupine in his groundhog-child disguise.

ళ   ళ   ళ

"Well," said the senior Fox Council member when hearing the story. "What do you think was written on that letter?"

115

"Precisely what we saw," said Soren. "I don't even know if it was enchanted. I suspect it was blank, but that he knew she would wish so hard for it to say whatever suited the situation, and she would. I suspect she knows it is blank too. But easier to believe it describes a son's plans to come back later on than to believe that your son can no longer write it," Soren paused to contemplate and second guess himself before speaking again. "But I don't know. Perhaps it was enchanted, and shared some secret that we'll never know. All I know is that whatever message it was meant to send, it seems to have been successful."

"So it is," said the Council Fox. "You see, Soren, people are going to deceive themselves one way or another, every day. There's no reason you can't get in between and make some good come of it. That's really the long and short of Fox Law, I think. People long for illusions. If we didn't provide them, they'd just find them somewhere else. And if it's all lies anyway, all imagination anyway, what difference does it make what the lie sounds like or the illusion looks like? None of it matters much."

The two sat for a bit. Soren felt his body slouch.

"Well, Soren," the fox council member said, "you did good work, even if you don't feel good about it. Keep this up and you may become a member of the council yet."

Soren wandered into the forest that night, drunk on Wolf Mead, staring at a blank piece of paper. It began to rain, and the paper slowly disappeared. He thought about what he would wish it to say, but it tore apart before he could make the writing appear.

He fell asleep in the rain, and when he woke up, he saw two branches lying on the ground, reached over, and tied them to his ears.

8. GO ASK MOKUM

Soren flinched and Sophie tensed up as a Wolf Union pack charged toward him, only to lick his fur clean of the ash that had collected. Soren was being groomed.[13] Sophie laughed in relief.

Soren smiled too, but shrugged them away.

"Sophie," he said suspiciously. "Didn't you fall into the sea?"

"There was a net."

There was a tense silence. Soren looked around at the wolves who seemed happy to see him.

"Why are you being nice to me?" he asked.

The wolves shrugged.

"You're an honest fox, so..." a small one said.

"You're one of us," said a German Shepard.

---

[13] *"Despite the diversity of morphology and ecology in members of the Canidae, social behavior remains similar throughout the Family. Some specializations have occurred in group-living species, serving to maintain group cohesion and to reduce intraspecific aggression, and these changes in behaviors and postures have been ones of degree rather than kind. The type of specialization differs in each species and is probably related to its ecology."* - *Devra G. Kleiman, Zoological Society of London, "Some Aspects of Social Behavior in the Canidae," American Society of Zoologists, 7:365-372 (1967).*

"I've already brought tragedy to one Phylum through impersonation," Soren said. "You shouldn't take me in. I'm not a wolf any more than she is."

The wolves looked confused.

"You should go see Mokum," the shepherd said. "He can give you some details about... your situation."

"I was trying to steal your mead," Soren said. "I was going to steal your mead and sell it to a badger."

"Do you want to bring your mead back to the badger?" asked the shepherd. Soren waited a moment.

"Not like this," he said.

"You got too close to the source, and you survived. You should have been killed by the mushroom. But now, I think it's important that you drink more of the mead, and then go to see Mokum."

"This is too much mead and too much adventure," said Soren. "I want to go home."

The wolves looked to one another. The raccoons were on their way, and maybe the foxes. There was only one place Soren could go, and it wasn't home. The Shepherd spoke.

"That's not a good idea."

"What?"

"Go see Mokum."

Soren, still coming down from a ledge of mushrooms and Wolf Mead, was oblivious that anyone was looking for him at all. His body, having just moved through a lifetime of trauma, was exhausted. He only wanted to sleep, and thought, briefly, of the dreams he might have: wearing pajamas back home in his Victorian, nibbling a tofu triangle in his study, reading a book that explained things with concrete certainty. He imagined curling up in a ball of his own fur, to sleep, and being interrupted by a knock on the door, surprised by a pack of angry foxes and wolves, raccoons with torches, and a badger demanding a bag of money.

Soren snapped back to the present and knew what he had to do.

"Is Mokum on the top of a mountain or something?"

"Yes."

Soren sighed.

0ft.

"Some creatures understand more than others about others," thought Soren.

100ft.

"The wisest creatures know about other Phylums the way the rest of us animals know about ourselves," he told Sophie.

They continued to climb.

200ft.

"The rarest of creatures see the world, at all of its levels, the way we know ourselves: the moss' relationship to the stone, but also, the relationship of the tiny creatures inside the moss, the interactions of the cells."

They continued to climb.

300ft.

"Some creatures, I imagine, might even know the way the spheres circle around each other. You know, Sophie, even you, you remember how to talk to things that I don't even remember to talk to. Did you know you can talk to the moon? Some creatures remember that they can talk to the moon!"

"Yes," said Sophie.

They continued to climb.

400ft.

"I guess, somewhere, I knew that there was a particular personality to the moon, and a particular personality to the cell in the moss, and then sometimes I'd remember. But even when I remembered, I couldn't tell anyone about it, because everyone had forgotten how to ask."

"You've forgotten the thing that the mushrooms know, but if you ask, they'll tell you why they reach outward from the tree when rain hits the bark," said Sophie.

They continued to climb.

500ft.

They continued to climb.

600ft.

"We've become a very lonely species," said Soren. They continued to climb. "I have become a very lonely species."

700ft.

They continued to climb.

800ft.

They continued to climb.

900ft.

Soren was sacked from the side by a blur of white fur. Teeth sunk into his side. The image of a white wolf obscured his vision; then his own red fur and red spirit on the animal's teeth. Soren's bone laid in the creature's mouth. Sophie stood still. Soren screamed for help, but Sophie stood, unmoved, then lowered her neck to lick some moisture from a tree stump.

Soren felt down where his bone was stolen; he could feel it was absent, but so was a scar. His fur, too, was intact.

"Did you see that?" said Soren.

"No," said Sophie. "You're drunk on Mushrooms and Wolf Mead."

They continued to climb.

100ft.

A bandaged and tailless Eldest Raccoon and Mr.
Buxton had formed a search party for Soren Fox,
Esquire, and had arrived at the mountain based on
testimony from a mortified and disloyal Lhasa Apso.

With the soil and the scrub in their nostrils, it
was easy to see where to go. The Eldest Raccoon
climbed in sad silence, and Mr. Buxton opted not to
break it.

1000ft.

"Every fox dreams about wolves," said Soren. "But we're terrified of being them. We can't bite, so we just talk instead, and lies are our teeth."

They rested.

1100ft.

"I remember a story that one of the Fox Council Elders would tell me, as a boy," Soren rambled. "It's an old story about two foxes who watched a raccoon alone on a boat in a storm. One fox wagers to another that the raccoon would drown before the storm lets out. The other fox accepts. They spend the rest of the storm outside, watching to see if the raccoon gets into port, or drowns. And so, this Fox Elder said, that was the sign of Fox Intelligence, the reason we ruled the city: We know that there's nothing to be done about other people's misery, but we still care enough to make a bet on the outcome."

"Did he drown?" asked Sophie.
"Who?"
"The raccoon."
"Oh," said Soren. "I have no idea."

They continued to climb.

1200ft

The only thing Soren could drink was more Wolf Mead, and so the fungus that he had already taken into his pores was being replenished. He felt his sweat connecting him to the Mariposas.

"That story tells me that we are the designers of mange," Soren said. "We don't clean ourselves because we can just make others think we are clean. We just let the parasites eat away at our skin, but I can see it now, you know. If I went back, we'd be a city of mangey foxes putting all the lemon and honey on our tea because it's delicious while it should go to heal our rotting skin."

They continued to climb.

1100ft.

The Eldest Raccoon stopped suddenly, having caught Sophie's eye in silent recognition. Mr. Buxton sensed something, but was unable to see her.

"Do you feel that, Mr. Buxton?"
"What?" Mr. Buxton took inventory of his sensations, and found nothing amiss.

The Eldest Raccoon had detected the slightest chill passing through tanoak leaves in trembling breezes, carrying some residue of feeling. The Eldest Raccoon had never met the spirits of truth and disenchantment, but he knew to let them work without bending them to his wishes-of-the-moment.

"Mr. Buxton, our chase is over," the Eldest Raccoon said. "I have a sense that the elusive fox will not be a problem for us anymore. Let's complete our mourning for the music we have lost, and in due time, let's gather up new instruments to sing new songs."

Mr. Buxton trusted the Eldest Raccoon, and simply nodded in agreement. He took his walking stick and the pair began to head back down the mountain.

1300ft.

Soren caught himself talking to nobody. Sophie had disappeared. There hadn't been a fuss, and then Soren remembered that she said she was going to stay where she was for a bit. Soren heard her but had kept talking anyway, he was on to something, and it was more important than acknowledging that Sophie was heading back.

That's when he saw Mokum. Mokum was a gray wolf larger than any dog Soren had ever seen. He was about the size of the sad buffalo that were stuck in the city after the human departure.

"You want a feast," Mokum told him.

"I suppose I do. I always love a feast."

"You want a round table with many people who love you, and a cornucopia that never stops dispensing fruits. A broken vending machine full of tofu triangles and raspberries."

Soren was silent. He didn't know where this was going.

"You want a table full of ghosts. It's all you have in your world."

"Your world seems to have more ghosts, per capita..."

"We have spirits. We have magic. Your magic is a book of rules you never stop writing. That's demon magic. Fox magic. And that's why we've locked you out."

"Locked... *us* out?"

"You foxes are quite proud of taking over that city and keeping it just like it was. You forget that the builders of that city are gone. They'd drained themselves so completely that they don't even haunt it."

"I don't see why we'd want to live in a haunted place."

"We don't live in a haunted place. We live in a place with living spirits. You know you've forgotten it. You climbed this hill, and you made it barely more than half way up. I had to meet you, as a favor, because as a fox you can't make it to the top of this mountain anymore. You've forgotten how to get to spirits. You're now precisely half-way between the world of human death and the world of living spirits. You chose to live in that city, and to never leave. Then you act like you're working to keep us out. We don't need your laws to survive. We are thriving here. Your civilization is death. Your laws are a prison. You come into the world – *our* world, the *real* one – and you don't trust it, you don't trust *us*. All that is left for you to do is commit to a human death. That's your crucible. Once your fox kind forgets how the rest of us die, you'll take their place. And once you do, the rest of us will be subject to your rule. That's why we've surrounded you. We want you to be safe. But we need to be safe from you."

Soren found all of this a bit hard to take. After all, he was a fox, and he wasn't out to rule the rest of the Phylums; it was hardly ever discussed in these terms at Fox Council.

"Have you ever *been* to a Fox Council meeting?" Soren asked. "They mostly talk about getting together for fox-jump games. They certainly aren't planning for global domination. We're just trying to keep to our own laws."

"Earlier on the mountain I ate your body. You woke up to the illusion of your fundamental physical integrity. Now I'm showing you your real disease: The illusion of your world view. You think like people thought. You collect experience and use it to shape the future. You never look at the world as it lays itself out to you, as a now."

Soren understood this to be true. He thought back to what he said before, about the creatures that knew that the moss had its own cells and the cells had their own spirit. Soren couldn't see the spirit of a clam if he was eating it; he couldn't hear the squirrels.

"You can't hear anything at all," Mokum said. "Because none of this is here for you. You are owed nothing. You are one meaningless part of a meaningless phylum on a meaningless spectrum of Animalia, an Animalia that has risen through mysterious coincidence on one small sphere among billions. And yet, you can only see the world through a lens of what it offers to you. It was humans and cats who did that before us, and next it will be foxes."

The scale of his consciousness against a landscape of infinitude was a lot to take for Soren, especially during a psychedelic mead binge. Paradoxically, Soren became incredibly terrified of his own death.

"I see it's too late," Mokum said. "You were the last of the honest foxes. Now all I've done is made it impossible for you to live without anxiety."

"I've been doing that pretty well without your help," Soren replied.

With that, a ferocious wind came, and Mokum was swallowed by the flung woodland debris of leaves and sticks. When the small tornado disappeared, he was gone.

"I went to see a human who was flat on a wall," said Sophie, who had been watching from some distance. "She delivered this poem, and I didn't understand it, but it sounds like what the wolf said. Do you want to hear it?"

"Yes," said Soren.

The Disillusioning Spell

The wine is sweet,
But the morning roils the belly.
Don't bite into the persimmon,
It is rotten and brown.
Fair is the scarlet flower
Of the death lily,
But why pick it?
Beauty? Wisdom? Love?
Don't be deceived.
They are threads in the fabric
Of the greatest lie
you've told yourself.

9. SOREN SETS NO PRECEDENTS

Soren, having received wisdom from a God on a mountaintop that he didn't want to listen to, was sure that his duty compelled him to return to the Fox Council and attempt to convert them to an annoying and depressing truth.

It undid all source of good in the world, Soren thought, to go about chattering about the meaninglessness of their lives and the illusion of superiority over the living kingdom. He imagined going and telling Peter about the visions he'd had of the red-ant sunshine fur and his atonement with his never-existing brothers. The conversation would get him nowhere.

But it was increasingly clear that he couldn't stay in the forest. Soren had never sunk his teeth into the sides of another creature for the sake of devouring it. The wolves hunted rabbits and squirrels, the two species that refused to participate in peace with wolves. Soren ate them, sure, but never hunted them. He asked if the wolves wouldn't mind catching them on his behalf in exchange for payment — he still had some money in his pockets — but the wolves didn't even bother to say no. The Border Collie tilted his head in confusion, and that was the end of it. Soren relied on berries and grasses, the things that seemed ever so pleased to be eaten.

The seasons changed, and the wolves would huddle to keep warm. Soren felt himself surrounded and swallowed by the fur of creatures he didn't know. If the red-ant vision was supposed to change him, it had only gone so far as to assure him that he was no wolf.

He stared to the sky, cold night air bringing stars pop in sharpest pinprick contrast. When he remembered to talk to the stars, he asked what sense did they make of his tiny shape among a huddle of tiny shapes? Soren felt himself wholly himself, and yet a blur, and then he fell to sleep.

Sophie had stayed for a few days, but being among wolves kept her on edge. She slowly started to move in wider circles in her foraging, and when the season of clearest nighttime stars had come, she found herself out by the stones on the border of the city, staring at the spot where the love she couldn't keep from sliding had finally been swallowed.

She knew, from her vision, that she had let go of the weight of the Deerstone, and it had meant an embrace of solitude. Her body could be light even if the soul within it was heavy. She enjoyed running, darting in graceful leaps over twisted and fallen wood in the forest. She had spoken the spirit of that weight, and finally understood the source of gravity pulling down from deep within the spheres. Each had a heavy burden, but danced through the skies after sunset. She began to see this lightness everywhere.

Birds darted; she leaped, clouds stayed suspended. If she moved with grace along the ground, she thought, it was a caress of the planet. The weight of that stone, the weight of lost love, the gravity of absence, were all absorbed into the cores of things, centering the spinning sphere allowed everything else to dance upon its surface without floating into space.

When the coldest season had passed, Sophie returned to Wolf Union with some news.

"The city has been destroyed," she told them.

Soren was incredulous. Scouts hadn't reported any changes, they didn't hear anything at all. Was this a fox trick? Were they luring him back?

Soren spent days trying to put it out of his mind. He spent his days tucking raspberries into tofu triangles, a pale imitation of his favorite foods, and it was this, of all things, that formed the final straw. Sitting and contemplating a return to get some fried tofu triangles, Soren thought how odd it was not to worry about returning. It was novel.

He asked if Sophie would take him back to the city, and together they walked, for 7 days, when they came upon the sacred vermillion towers of the crossing bridge, immersed, as almost always, in fog.

Without speaking, they each turned their backs, looking to wilderness. In the distance, the boats of the Raccoon Grotto clanged their bells. Soren turned back to the sacred bridge, clapped his hands, bowed deeply, then clapped again. The fog gave its permission, and the two entered the gauzy mist.

જ   જ   જ

Indeed, the city was black and brown. The buildings had rotted, as if ten times their age; the streets were broken with maws full of water and garbage. The wire-poles had fallen, some buildings had collapsed completely. It smelled like corpses and urine.

In the distance, a fox called out to him.

"Rip Van Winkle!" he called to Soren. "You've awakened!"

"What's happened here?" Soren asked.

"Well, Soren, you may find this hard to believe, but we've gotten on just fine without you. Nothing's changed at all. I'm sure that's terribly disappointing news."

The fox was covered in mange, patches of missing fur revealing pink skin scratched red in some places. Tufts of red hair emerged from small tears in fabric over his knees and elbows.

"I'm reluctant to ascribe this all to one winter away, but you won't convince me that this is all exactly as I've left it. The city looks like you've been at war."

"Nothing compared to living in a fucking wolf heap, is it? Here comes Soren Fox Esquire, the world's only antlered fox-dog jazz man. Don't forget to wash your teeth-shredded rabbit before you eat it, raccoon-wolf. Or do you only eat berries now, like your friend here?"

"You're the world's cleverest fox, I assure you," said Soren, "But you're annoying me more than insulting me. Is Peter somewhere?"

"Sure, he's where he always is."

Soren and Sophie moved through the rubble of the city until Sophie stopped.

"What is it?" asked Soren.

"I don't know." Sophie nodded toward a small pile, three feet in front of her. Rising from the brown and mulchy leaves was a small skeleton.

"Is it a dead fox?" asked Sophie.

Soren inspected it. "The snout is all wrong."

"It's a cat," Sophie said.

Soren frowned.

"How do you know?" he asked.

"I asked her."

They clapped, bowed, and clapped again, giving rest to anything left of the spirit inside the bones. But soon they encountered another ape-like corpse in the steel belly of a rusted-out automobile. It seemed to them that the humans had re-appeared, en masse, as deteriorated bodies. They tried to ask it, but the humans weren't about to start talking now.

They tried to perform the ceremony, but soon they saw bodies everywhere, cats and people alike, scattered across the landscape in such numbers that they would never be able to walk.

"Humans don't need the ceremony anyhow," Soren said. Sophie agreed, but sadly.

When they arrived at the Fox Council Den, it stood in stark contrast to the world around it. Its steel shape was impeccably preserved, and the stained-glass windows seemed to produce light. Even the fog seemed to lift.

They walked across the courtyard to the large wooden door and pushed it open. The same interior beckoned back with a familiar air of power. Books filled wooden shelves, all facing the carving of a human body, arms open, flying to heaven, the symbol of the human departure that the Fox Council had always kept in its memory.

Peter was one of the few foxes in the building, writing out laws into books. Some younger foxes pushed carts of books to place them on the appropriate shelf.

"Soren?" Peter asked. "You've finally come back."

Soren was caught off guard. Peter seemed happy to see him. It took a minute to see that what Peter was nervous.

"Things here seem to be holding up without me," said Soren. "I wish I could say the same for the rest of the city."

Peter stared a bit, expressionless. "Yes," he started.

"What happened outside?"

"Oh that, that's nothing," Peter said.

Soren was confused. He couldn't tell if Peter was hiding something, or oblivious.

"There's cat skeletons," Soren said. Everyone in the building turned to look at him. "And dead people."

Silence.

"The city is full of cat skeletons and dead people," Soren said once more, this time forcefully.

"Says the fox with the antlers," said one of the young book-cart pushing foxes. The others with the carts snickered.

None of the fox council members laughed.

"Junior council, can you leave the chambers, please?" Peter asked. They stopped what they were doing and, with furrowed foreheads, made their way to other parts of the building.

"Tell us about your vision, Soren."

"It's not a vision. It's plain as day. Come on outside, you can see it for yourself."

Outside, Soren gestured to a bustling row of well-preserved Victorian homes with steel and concrete pillars holding up the sky.

"It's all ruined," he said. "What's happened?"

"Nothing at all, Soren. It's just as it was when you left. I mean, some of the badger bars have gotten more expensive."

Soren grew frustrated. He looked at Sophie.

"I see it," said Sophie. "It's real."

Soren looked around, pawing through the soot for a cat's skull. He picked it up, and showed it to them. "See?" he said. They looked at his hands and saw a round white stone.

"A white rock," said Peter.

Frustrated, Soren looked to the stained-glass window. With all the strength he had, he tossed the skull through the window of the council chambers. The foxes followed it with their heads, and the glass body of a departed human shattered, a hole taking the place of a flaming heart.

Peter shouted.

"That's it Soren. You could have broken that window. You've gone completely mad, and I'm locking you up until you recover from whatever magic you've been hostage to, or reveal the goal of any trick you're playing."

"I DID break the window!" Soren shouted.

The Council pounced, and Sophie jumped to his aid, swirling her antlers toward the rush. She leapt through the air, again remembering the lightness of her body, the gravity of hooves against the concrete. The wrapping of her body around her spirit had always felt like a prison. With the swipe of a fox blade, her body opened. The hoof fell from the air, back to the planet, and the rest of her crashed behind it.

Soren, stunned, was wrestled to the ground, and a stone brought to the back of his head. He awoke in a cage surrounded by darkness.

He struggled to see anything in his surroundings that he could talk to. This was a human cage, there was no spirit to talk to.

Soren struggled to sit upright. He had just enough room to squat. Alone, in darkness, he felt the hollowness of the world. He wished for Sophie; she wouldn't come, couldn't come. He wished for his brothers, before remembering they had never existed. His mother had never known him. His father had replaced him. His colleagues had denied what he could see so clearly. He had turned his back to the wolves who had tried to welcome him, had betrayed the raccoons that welcomed him into their community.

Soren began to weep for the absence of all these things. He wept heavy and easy tears. There was not even a city he could love. Home, what was it? He would never know. It had never been there. He wept until his body surged with relief, as if his body had to intervene out of pity. Drained, and exhausted, he stopped sobbing and stared out, to the darkness, to the absence of everything.

His sobbing turned into a scream. If everything we do stems from a desire to return home — a home all the way back, before we ever learned to speak, before, maybe, we ever even existed — there is terror in it. His scream was one of true fear, but also an act of resistance to the impossible task of living through our own dream, the horror that we will never be alive enough to live through our own death. Soren had been born into a darkness that could never be released through unity with his brothers, or through his own capacity for destruction.

And he remembered he could talk to *that*.

৵ ৵ ৵

What am I, Soren? That gray silence that wraps around a home at dusk, when you sit across from the people you love with nothing to say? What is it that you think I bring? Don't you remember that when you have been most alone, and have gripped your abandonment tight around your heart; it was me that reminded you of the solitude squeezing the heart of *all* things? When you, a fox, are too good for wolves, I reminded you that there is no difference where I am. You are all distinct, and cursed with yearning. Don't you ever see the secret city between things? I am the path that takes all lonely things to each other. Every heart is broken, and sadness seeps into every crack of every heart.

I am the texture of honey. And your hearts are immersed in me. I'm here, seeping into your wound, but where do I end? Nowhere; like night, like light,

I'm bound to you, and to everyone who lives, and I fill the space between you. I connect everything to everyone. You never ask me questions, so you never hear what I come to tell you. Your sadness at being isolated from this world is what you share with everything else that lives within it.

∾   ∾   ∾

Soren waited patiently for three days for someone to arrive. He knew they would, and it was just inconvenient for them to wait so long. They were wasting their time and his.

The lights came on. Finally, Peter came.

"Soren, have you settled down?"

"Yes. Tell me something. Do you know that I'm telling the truth?"

Peter was silent. He sat down, in front of Soren.

"There is nothing written in Fox Law that is compatible with what you say," said Peter. "So it cannot be true."[14]

"What if something exists that transcends Fox Law?"

"It's possible. But for us to know it, we'd have to write it into Fox Law, or else the whole system falls to pieces. And Fox Law has kept things very reliable. It keeps the rubbish going out every Tuesday, so the raccoons can eat. Even the creatures

---

[14] *A certain element of comic relief can be felt in Peter's immediate project (announced even while the vision was before his eyes) to convert the ineffable into a stone foundation. Only six days before, Jesus had said to him: "Thou art Peter, and upon this rock I will build my church," then a moment later, "thou savorest not the things that be of God, but those that be of men" (Matthew 16:18, 23)" - Joseph Campbell, Hero With a Thousand Faces, page 230.*

you go and live with. You're smart enough to know by now that Wolf Law is formed from Fox Law, just as the deer learned to sprint faster because a wolf comes to hunt it." Peter looked away for a minute. "Sorry to mention her."

"So, you know it's true."

"What I know are the rules that govern this little experiment, and that we have them to protect ourselves from the desperate existence of those beyond the city. I also understand that you think you're going to shatter the rule of law, and reveal some law-beyond-law that will liberate everyone into your own personal brand of existential despair.

That's very kind of you, Soren — that was sarcasm — and you may think that we're afraid of you. But we aren't. We know that given the choice between your world and this one, people will choose the one without corpses in the street. We know that there were some like you, among the humans, and that they caused all kinds of problems. It's not really your brand of truth that we're afraid of getting out.

It's the consequences of people believing it. It's the anger and frustration and bloodshed that comes when people pretend they know what you mean."

Soren thought for a long time. Peter let him.

"I want to show you something," Peter said. "But then you must promise to leave, and not come back here, or else stay and live your life like you always had."

Soren couldn't think of any third option he would prefer to those two, and was relieved that it meant he wasn't going to die.

"Sure," he said.

A rotted orange.

They walked up a flight of stairs, past the council chambers, to a gold door. Peter reached into a box and revealed a moldy, imploded fruit of some sort. "An orange," he said. He opened the door with a key, exposing a staircase with red carpet winding in an upward spiral.

At the top of the stairs, another door. Peter stopped, clapped, bowed, rose, and clapped. He gestured to Soren to do the same. Then, Peter took an orange out of his jacket, tossing it into the air as if to feel its weight. It was bright orange, as if bursting with sweetness.

They opened the door and there, in a beautiful room of stone and glass bookshelves, was a white fox with nine tails, collared and chained.

"What happens now?" asked Soren. But Peter had left and locked the door behind him.

The Nine Tailed Fox replied,

"

."

Soren did not understand.

X. SOPHIE LONGS FOR THE HERD

Sophie awoke in the dark space, immediately met with the sound of a vast and intimate herd rising from the distance. As the storm came closer, her legs bolted forward, and her body dissolved into the running collective of distinct but identical beings, each hoof a part of a joyous stampede, moving together toward some unknown and distant darkness.

END

ABOUT THE AUTHOR

Eryk Salvaggio lives in San Francisco, California.

OWL COLLECTORS CLUB

Owl Collectors Club is an independent publishing house specializing in art books and collage.

For more titles, find us online at:

www.owlcollectors.club

IMAGE CREDITS

Soren Fox, Esquire: Collage by Eryk Salvaggio. Fox image from "Dogs, Jackals, Wolves and Foxes: A Monograph of the Canidae," p186, original woodcut by JG Keulemans, 1890. Published 1890 by RH Porter, London.

Sophie: From "An Introduction to the Study of Mammals, Living and Extinct," p328, by William Henry Flower and Richard Lydekker. Published 1891 by A and C Black, London. Artist unknown.

Eldest Raccoon: From "The Land and Sea Mammals of Middle America and the West Indies," p94, by Daniel Giraud Elliot. Published 1904, Field Columbian Museum Publications of Chicago. Artist unknown.

Sequoia Tree: From "Elementary Physical Geometry," p330, by Jacques Wardlaw Redway. Published 1908, C. Scribner and Sons, New York. Artist Unknown.

A fire in the forest: From "Wild Sports in the Far West," p215, by Friedrich Gerstacker. Published 1859, Crosby Nicholas and Co., Boston. Original crayon drawing by Harrison Weir.